Ballerina Dreams

Ballerina Dreams

Ballet Magic

Ann Bryant

USBORNE

The publisher would like to thank
Sara Matthews of the Central School of Ballet
for her assistance.

This collection first published in the UK in 2006 by Usborne Publishing Ltd,
Usborne House, 83-85 Saffron Hill, London EC1N 8RT, England.
www.usborne.com

Cover photograph by Ray Moller.
Illustrations by Tim Benton.

A CPI catalogue record for this title is available
from the British Library.

UK ISBN 9780746077344
First published in America in 2007.AE
American ISBN 9780794517403
JFMA JJASOND/07
Printed in India.

Contents

Poppy's Secret Wish

My sincerest thanks to Victoria Zafiropoulous
– Miss Victoria, the Principal of Tenterden Ballet Studio
– for her invaluable help, and for providing me with
inspiration for the character of Miss Coralie.
My thanks, also, to Rufina Hunn for her very astute help,
and to Sara Matthews, the Assistant Director of the Central School
of Ballet, for kindly allowing us to watch some classes.
And most of all, my thanks to Megan Larkin for
believing in me.

1 Desperate to be Picked

Hi! I'm Poppy. I'm ten years old and I've got red hair and freckles. I'm the only one with red hair in my whole ballet class. You can't see much of it, thank goodness, by the time I've scraped it back and put on my ballet hairband. I wish I could scrape my freckles back too. That's only a small wish though. I don't mind them all that much actually. My big wish is *much* more important.

"Why do you look so worried, Poppy?" Mom was looking at me in the rearview mirror.

"Because I *am* worried. Miss Coralie's going

to tell us who's taking the test today. What if she doesn't pick me?"

My heart was doing the little skipping thing it does when I'm nervous. Just thinking about Miss Coralie makes me get jittery.

"I'm sure you'll be fine."

"She might not think I'm good enough, though."

"Then you can do it next time. It doesn't matter, does it? What's the rush?"

Mom didn't understand. She knows I really like ballet. In fact, she knows I *love* it. But she doesn't realize that it's the most important thing in my whole life. She's got no idea that I dream of being the best in my class and getting picked to go to a real ballet school – even though I know it could never happen in a gazillion years.

And she doesn't know that sometimes I practice in my bedroom when I'm supposed to be asleep. I lie on top of the quilt and stretch my legs till it hurts.

I'd like to be as flexible as Tamsyn Waters. She can do the splits front ways and sideways, and she can also lie on her stomach and curl herself backward so her feet touch her nose. She's kind of a show-off.

Everyone knows that Tamsyn is sure to be picked for the test, and then she'll go up to the next class with Jasmine.

"But I want to get into grade five, Mom. I don't want to be left behind because I'm not good enough."

"It doesn't mean you're not good enough if you don't get picked, Poppy," said Mom carefully. "It just means that you're not quite ready and that you'll probably be able to do it next time instead...or the time after."

I sighed. "That'll take forever! And anyway, it would mean I'm not good enough, because Miss Coralie keeps telling us that it's not only about how well we've learned the steps, it's about our whole attitude toward ballet, and how much we practice and what our overall achievement is."

Mom was looking very serious. No wonder. There was nothing she could say because I'd told the absolute truth and if I wasn't picked it meant I wasn't good enough. Period.

And, actually, it would feel like the end of my whole life. Nobody understands that because it's secret. Well, nobody except Jasmine Ayed. She's my friend from ballet.

Thinking about Jasmine made a little burst of words come zipping up my body and out of my mouth. "I can't wait till afterward!"

Mom gave me a big smile in the mirror. "I'd better go home and start fixing something to eat when I've dropped you off, hadn't I? If Jasmine gets half as hungry as you do after ballet classes, it's not going to be easy fitting all the food on the table!"

I felt kind of like a baby when Mom said that. She doesn't usually talk to me as if I'm a baby.

I think she was just trying to keep my mind off this big important day. But it didn't work.

"I won't be in the same class as Jasmine if I don't get chosen, you know," I said. I knew I was whining, sort of. I couldn't help it.

"Miss Coralie might decide to keep you both in grade four, since you're so much younger than all the others."

"She won't keep Jasmine down, I bet."

"Well even if she doesn't, you'll still see each other."

"Not as much. It's not like we go to the same school, you know."

"Well..." Mom's eyes were darting around now. She was looking for a parking space. "I'll just pull in here, honey. Now, don't go getting yourself all worked up or you won't do your best." She turned and gave me what I call her firm smile.

I got out of the car and ran, with my dark blue bag banging against my side, to the big, heavy door of The Coralie Charlton School of Ballet.

"Good luck!"

I barely heard Mom's voice because of the noise of the traffic on High Street. Then I pushed open the door.

The smell of the entrance to the ballet school is the strongest smell I've ever smelled in a building – even stronger than the lunchroom at school. I don't really know what it is, but it always makes me think about an old castle that might have Rapunzel or someone imprisoned in it. The walls are cold and gray and it's sort of dark and dirty.

Your footsteps make a splitching, echoing sound when you run upstairs. I know there's no such word as splitching, but it's the best way to describe the noise. It's a spiral staircase, only with corners instead of bends, and it goes on and on and on. It's wonderful when you've passed the first two corners and you start to hear the voices of the other students up in the changing room. You can also hear the piano. It sounds plinky-plonky at first, but then it turns into a recognizable tune when you get nearer the top. It reminds me of a flower opening.

"Poppy!"

I leaned over the railing and saw Jasmine coming through the door down below. "Hi!" I called. "I'm really nervous. Are you?"

She nodded and her eyes looked all black and huge. "I couldn't find my tights and I thought Mom might have forgotten to wash them."

"Oh, no! Where were they?"

She giggled. "In my drawer. Same as usual." Then her voice got breathless because she was running up the steps so fast. "I must be going blind."

As Jasmine ran, her ponytail swung from side to side and spread out at the bottom like an upside-down fan. I'd give anything to have beautiful black hair like Jasmine's. In fact, I wish I could swap looks with Jasmine altogether.

Her skin is dark with not a freckle in sight. Jasmine says she'd rather look like me, but I know she only says it to make me feel better.

The moment she reached me, she clutched my arm. "We can practice for the test when we get to your house after class, can't we?"

The jitters jolted my stomach when she said that, and they danced around and around as we climbed the last few stairs. "What if I'm not picked, Jasmine?"

"You *will* be. You're good."

"Not as good as you."

"Yes, you are."

"I'm not. It's so obvious."

"Well, *I* think you are."

"Well, Miss Coralie doesn't."

"It doesn't matter what Miss Coralie thinks. *She* is only an ex-Royal Ballet dancer. *I'm* the important one around here!" We both began to giggle. But Jasmine stopped immediately. We were nearly at the changing room.

"Oh, no!"

"What?"

"That's the *révérence* music, isn't it?"

Jasmine pronounced *"révérence"* the French way. It's the name of the curtsy step that you do at the end of the lesson. Her eyes were all big again because she thought the class before ours was just finishing and we were going to be late. But I recognized the music.

"It's okay, it's the other class's dance. We've got plenty of time."

I knew I sounded like someone who doesn't ever worry about *anything*, but inside me the jitters were spreading like crazy. I was about to open the changing-room door when Jasmine whispered, "Good luck, Poppy."

She gave me a thumbs-up sign and I gave her one back. Then we held out our hands, pressed our thumbs together, and closed our eyes. We always do this. It's our secret wishing signal.

"Please, please, *please* let us both be chosen," said Jasmine.

I said it too, with every single part of my whole body, inside and out.

There were lots of girls getting changed, and one or two were eating potato chips and doing *pliés.*

Tamsyn Waters was stretching right in the middle of the room. She was in a crab position. "Hi, Poppy! Hi, Jasmine!"

"How did you know it was us?" asked Jasmine.

Tamsyn uncurled smoothly and looked at herself in the mirror. "I recognized your feet." Then she arched one of her own feet and I saw a proud little smile go across her face.

Jasmine gave me a quick look. We both hate it when Tamsyn shows off about how limber she is.

"Oh, *no!*" screeched a girl called Sophie Cottle. "I can't get this bump out of my hair. I'll have to start all over again!" Sophie's got very thick hair and it's layered, so it's practically impossible to make it lie flat and stay in place under her hairband. "Has anyone got any spare hairpins?"

I handed her a few hairpins from the inside pocket of my bag, and felt happy that my hair is so long and fine. It only turns curly a little at the bottom, so it's easy to bunch up into a bun. Mia, a friend in my class at school, says that where she goes for ballet lessons they can wear their hair loose if they want. That's because hers is the kind of dance school where they do modern dancing and tap dancing and things like that, and mine's more of a traditional ballet school. Even its name sounds traditional – The Coralie Charlton School of Ballet. Students do ballet until the age of sixteen, and one or two girls have even gotten into the Royal Ballet School from here.

When I'd gotten changed, and had my shoes on neatly, and made sure every strand of my hair was tucked right inside my hairband, I whispered, "Want to wait in the hall?"

Jasmine nodded and we sneaked out of the changing room. I really wanted to get warmed up before the class started today. Then I'd be able to show Miss Coralie my very best steps right from the beginning of class. That might make her notice me and think I'd be good enough for the test.

I could have warmed up in the changing room, I know, but I didn't want anyone to see me. Otherwise they'd all be thinking, *Look at Poppy Vernon! She must be absolutely* desperate *to qualify for the test.* Then, if Miss Coralie didn't pick me, everyone would probably stare at me and I'd turn bright red and feel like bursting into tears.

"Are my feet rolling?" I asked Jasmine, as I went into a *plié* in first position.

She looked at them carefully, then shook her head. "Are mine?"

"You never roll, Jazz. I *so* wish I was as good as you."

"I'm only good at some things. I'm not half as good as you at actual dancing. Miss Coralie always says you've got lovely expression."

"She's talking about my top half."

"No, I'm sure she means all of you."

I was just about to say *I bet she doesn't*, when I heard the *révérence* music coming from behind the closed door of Room One.

"They're finishing! Help! I'm scared, Jasmine!" I hissed.

And at the very same moment, the changing room door opened and all the others came out into the corridor. Jasmine and I did a quick thumb-thumb, down by our sides, where no one could see. Then we started to line up beside the door, first Jasmine, then me, then Tamsyn behind me.

"Why did you two come out here so early?" Tamsyn whispered into the back of my neck.

I turned my head and mouthed, "Just did," sort of shrugging at the same time.

Everyone knows you have to be in a silent line ready to file in the moment the other class has filed out.

The girls from the class before us came out looking hot and tired. They didn't talk as they went past us. Miss Coralie doesn't have a rule about that. It's just better to wait till you get into the changing room. Then you can talk to your friend about how bad you were or how you didn't understand something.

I noticed that Jasmine was standing in fifth position. She always looks like a real ballerina. I tried it out, but I felt stupid because it doesn't suit me and my body, standing like that. That's because I haven't got such a good natural turnout as Jasmine. In fact, I haven't got such a good *anything* as her. Especially brains. When we learn a sequence of steps, Jasmine can remember it right away but it takes me forever.

Desperate to be Picked

I suddenly realized I was standing between a really smart girl and a really flexible girl. And what am *I* good at? Nothing. Except expression, and I'm sure that doesn't count half as much. It had probably been a waste of time getting extra warmed up, because Miss Coralie would never pick me for the test. I was suddenly so depressed, I felt like turning my feet inward, rounding my shoulders, sticking my stomach out and dropping my head onto my chest.

"Come in, next class!"

This was it. The moment had arrived.

I stretched up tall, pulled my shoulders back and made a wish: *Please please please let me be picked.*

2 The New Girl

We always come in running with really light steps and go straight to a place at the *barre*. As I followed Jasmine, I noticed out of the corner of my eye that Miss Coralie was wearing her black swirly skirt, pale blue top, black leotard and white tights. She had her black shoes on, the ones with little heels that looked like ordinary, flat ballet shoes on the top. I'm not sure how old she is – a little older than Mom, I think. But she doesn't look like a mother. She looks... just perfect.

She was talking to Mrs. Marsden, the pianist,

but half-watching us at the same time. When we were all at the *barre*, she broke into a big smile and stood in first position with her back perfectly straight. Then she let the smile go around the whole room, so it seemed as if she was smiling at each of us.

"Good afternoon, girls," she said, putting her hand on an imaginary *barre* and lifting her chin a little. "*Pliés*. Fifth position..."

Mrs. Marsden was watching Miss Coralie carefully, waiting for the words: *Preparation...* and... Every single ballet exercise begins with these words. It's like a signal for Mrs. Marsden to play the first note of the music and for us to be ready to start the exercise immediately.

We were all standing up as straight and tall as telephone poles, staring at the back of the head of the girl in front, waiting for the magic words. But, instead of saying "*Preparation...* and..." Miss Coralie suddenly frowned and looked quickly around. "I thought the new girl was joining us today. Isn't she here?"

"New girl?" everyone whispered. "What new girl?"

I saw an impatient look cross Miss Coralie's face. "A girl called Rose Bedford is joining the class. Has anyone seen her?"

Everyone shook their heads and I heard Tamsyn whisper, "Never heard of her."

I'd heard of her though. She goes to my school. In fact, she's in the same grade as me, only not the same class. She's always getting in trouble with the teachers and she sings really loudly in assembly. She often forgets her coat, but she doesn't seem to notice that it's cold when she's racing around the playground with the boys.

As more and more pictures of Rose Bedford came into my head, I realized that the new girl couldn't possibly be the one I knew. There's no way the Rose Bedford from *my* school would ever do something like ballet. For one thing, she wouldn't be able to keep still long enough.

Miss Coralie glanced at her watch and frowned. Then she said briskly, "Well, we can't wait any longer," and right when no one was expecting it, suddenly said the magic words, "*Preparation...and...*"

I think it surprised Mrs. Marsden, because her hands flew to the piano and she looked flustered. She was barely in time with the *plié* music.

"...*one* and *two* and *rise* and *lower*..." went on Miss Coralie. She always counted and talked in the rhythm of the music. "And *turnout more* and *arm* and *head* and *again* and *two* and *three* and *four* and..."

My legs felt very strong, and I concentrated with all my might on turning out well and not rolling my feet. I couldn't tell if Miss Coralie had noticed my *pliés* yet, because she was behind me, but when we turned to face the other way I could see that she was watching Immy Pearson and Lottie Carroll. Immy and Lottie are really good at ballet. It was obvious that Miss Coralie was going to let *them* take the test, because her head was tipped to one side. She always does that when she thinks someone's doing well.

As she walked along the *barre* and drew nearer to me, I pulled my stomach in even tighter and turned my legs out as far as they would go. We were doing the *pliés* facing the other way now.

"And *one* and *two* and *very* nice, *Poppy*, and *five* and *six* and *seven* and *eight*."

The inside of my body started zinging. I was so happy. Miss Coralie had said my name before anyone else's. I tried with all my might to keep the smug look off my face, because I always hate that look when I see it on other girls' faces.

"*Battements tendus*," said Miss Coralie. (All the names of the exercises are in French. That one sounds like *batter mon tarn due*!)

"*Preparation* and..."

When the music started, I felt as though I could do anything. My feet were pointed, my knees were pulled up tight. "Good, Jasmine…"

That made me even happier. Jasmine and I were the only two in the whole class to have been mentioned so far. I don't know if I stopped concentrating for a second because I was so happy but, next thing I knew, Miss Coralie was moving my arm and then my hand. "You look like a wooden soldier, Poppy. Curve it gently…" I really tried to make it curve, but I knew it wasn't working. Miss Coralie got hold of my hand and flapped my arm. "What's this old chicken wing? Hmm?"

I heard a little snicker from behind me and tried to stop my face turning pink. Then I lifted my elbow and dropped my shoulder and… "*Lovely*, Poppy, *three* and *four* and…"

Whew!

✳

By the end of the *barre* work, I felt really tired because I'd been focusing so hard on trying to get everything exactly right. I'm never normally tired in ballet lessons. In fact, the only time I ever feel tired in my whole life is in the morning when Mom wakes me up!

For the center work, away from the *barre*, we always stand in rows. Miss Coralie tells you which row she wants you in. She put me in the third one, and Jasmine in the second. First we did *port de bras*, which are the arm movements. This is my favorite part of the whole lesson. The music reminds me of slow motion skiing on silver snow with a golden sky.

I was in my own little world, so it gave me a shock when the door suddenly opened. It's such an unusual thing to happen in the middle of a class that we all stopped what we were doing to turn around and stare. Even Mrs. Marsden stopped playing the piano.

"Ah, Rose," said Miss Coralie.

3 Please Let it Be Me

I nearly gasped out loud. It *was* the Rose Bedford from my school. Only you could hardly recognize her with her hair all scraped back under her hairband. The trouble was she'd pulled the hairband too far forward, so it pressed her eyebrows downward. And that made her look as though she was scowling. Her leotard was wrinkled around her stomach because it was too big for her, and her legs looked strange too, but I couldn't think why that was at first.

I looked at Jasmine to see what she was thinking and then I realized what was wrong with Rose's legs. It was the way she was standing, with her knees locked straight back, and her feet pointing straight ahead, which is the worst way to stand in ballet. Two girls in the row behind me were grinning, nearly giggling. Everyone else just seemed to be staring.

It felt like ages before Miss Coralie spoke, but actually it must have only been about two seconds. "Hello, Rose. We have already started."

Rose just nodded and took a couple of steps forward.

Miss Coralie used her brisk voice. "Is your mother with you?"

"She's gone now. Her car was in an illegal space."

Miss Coralie smiled then. "Oh, I see. Is that why you're late? Did your mother have trouble parking?"

"Not really – it just took forever to do my hair and everything."

I was surprised when Rose said that. It didn't look as though she'd brushed her hair at all. She had cowlicks sticking out of the top.

Miss Coralie's eyes widened. "Right. Well, let's continue, now that you're here," she said rather sharply. You'll be in the third row, Rose. Next to Poppy Vernon."

I moved to make space and that's when Rose noticed me.

"Hi!" She grinned.

"Hi," I said in a whisper.

"Do you know Poppy, Rose?" asked Miss Coralie.

I could feel everyone's eyes on me now.

"She goes to my school," said Rose, bending her knees and pulling at the bottom of her leotard.

Someone behind me snorted and I almost felt sorry for Rose because it was obvious her underwear was uncomfortable and she was trying to pull it straight.

"What?" said Rose, turning around and giving the girl behind her a dark look.

"Nothing," said the girl quickly.

"Can we continue, please?" said Miss Coralie, her eyes flashing. "Rose, I know you haven't taken ballet before, but in your audition I had the feeling that you could be very good if you work hard. That's the only reason I let you come join this class. So you need to concentrate really hard from now on. We don't allow talking in class because there isn't time for it. Just keep an eye on me or one of the girls in front of you, and you'll start to pick things up. It'll take time and, as I told you before, you'll have to do some practice at home. All right?"

Rose nodded, but I could tell that she wasn't really listening. She was staring around the room and still fiddling with the bottom of her leotard.

The silver-snow music didn't sound so magical after that, and I didn't do the rest of the *port de bras* as well as usual because I kept on wondering what Rose was doing. When we turned to face the corner, I could see her shoulders all stiff and her legs bent wrong. Miss Coralie didn't correct her at all because she was watching the rest of us so carefully.

Next it was the *adage*, which you pronounce *add-arge*. You have to have good balance for this section. Miss Coralie was going through the step with her back to us, so we could see exactly which leg we were supposed to use, when Rose suddenly started flailing her arms around like a windmill.

"I'm really stiff from all that slow stuff," she explained to me in a whisper.

"You're not supposed to talk," I mouthed back.

Miss Coralie turned around at that moment and frowned at me. "Are you watching, Poppy?"

I nodded hard and tried not to turn red. Angry thoughts began to whirl around inside my head, stopping me from concentrating the way I should. It wasn't fair.

"Facing me...fifth position *croisé*... And..." Miss Coralie didn't count this time. Just watched us hard. "I can't see your face, Sophie. Lovely, Lottie. Tighten the supporting knee, Poppy."

Rose turned around to look at my knee. Then she turned back and stuck her leg up really high at the back, only with a bent supporting leg and her shoulders all stiff. Miss Coralie corrected her and told her how to work at her *arabesques* at home. But I couldn't imagine Rose ever practicing at home. It just didn't seem like a Rose thing to do.

After the *adage* section, we moved on to the jumps.

"I'm looking for pointed toes and no bending forward!" said Miss Coralie briskly.

"Oh, goody," said Rose.

One or two girls giggled, while Immy Pearson gave me a look as if to say: *What a weirdo friend you've got.*

I wasn't sure whether to give her the same look back, so I just pretended to ignore her.

We did lots of jumps, but I don't think I did them very well. The problem was that I could still see Rose out of the corner of my eye. She was ruining my concentration by jumping really high. Her toes were pointed and her knees were straight but she wasn't keeping her arms in the right position at all. She was just trying to leap as high as she could. I tried to make myself ignore her, but it was no good.

It was really strange that Rose had come to The Coralie Charlton School of Ballet at all. I couldn't figure out why she didn't go to a modern dance class somewhere. I wondered if I'd dare to ask her afterward, but I didn't *really* want to talk to her because I kept remembering how scary she was at school, playing with boys and getting in trouble all the time.

She didn't fit in at Miss Coralie's for sure.

And I know it's horrible of me, but I didn't want her here, either.

After the jumps, came the most difficult part of the whole class: the steps. First we do the set steps, but after that Miss Coralie makes up a whole string of steps and puts them together in a sequence. It's supposed to be good training for when we're older. She gives us a new sequence of steps every two weeks. The first week, we learn the sequence and the second week we "polish it" as she calls it.

I'm terrible at remembering a whole sequence of steps by myself. Usually it doesn't matter, because I just go home and practice like crazy. Then at least I'm practically perfect by the time it's the next lesson. But today was different. Today I wanted to get it right immediately. The biggest jitters of all went whizzing around my body because I knew that, to get picked for the test, you have to be good at every single part of the lesson. I was glad Jasmine was in the row in front, so I could copy her.

Miss Coralie told us the steps slowly and carefully and I really tried my super best to remember them all. But while she was reeling off the long list of French words, all I could hear was Rose making little noises beside me: "Huh? What?"

"Okay, I'm going to give you a minute to try out the whole sequence on your own, while I have a quick word with Mrs. Marsden. Then we'll do it with the music. Rose, just do the best you can by copying the others."

A minute! That wasn't very long. I knew I had to work fast.

But Rose was hissing in my ear. "What's she talking about? Can you show me?"

"Actually, you should copy someone else," I whispered back. "I'm not very good at steps."

After that, I didn't have time to see what Rose was doing. I was concentrating too hard on learning the sequence myself. Jasmine was working it out right in front of me, so I just watched her and tried to follow everything she did.

"See, you *are* good at it!" Rose whispered. She was giving me a big friendly smile. "Especially the way you do that jumping thing where you have to cross your feet over."

I really wished she'd leave me alone because I hadn't gotten it right yet.

"Okay, everyone. Let's try it with the music. We'll start with the back row for a change."

My heart thumped and the jitters started to make me feel sick. We were doing it a row at a time! There was no way I'd be able to do it without Jasmine or at least *someone* to copy.

"And *one* and *two* and *three* and *four*..."

The back row was really good. No wonder, with Immy and Lottie in it.

"Hey, they're better than us, aren't they?" said Rose.

I nodded miserably.

"Well done, back row! Now let's have the third row, please."

Jasmine gave me a thumbs-up as I walked on shaky legs to my place.

"And…"

I thought I'd be able to do the first part at least, but even that went wrong. It was because I could see Rose out of the corner of my eye and I knew she was trying to copy me, but she just looked like a grasshopper. And, as soon as I'd thought that, I really lost my concentration. Then I heard Tamsyn giggling and I wasn't sure if it was because of me or because of Rose. It was all right for Rose. She didn't care. She wouldn't be doing the test anyway. But it was very important for me and now I'd completely messed it up *and* I'd turned red.

Watching Jasmine's row and the front row made me even more miserable, because nearly everyone was better than me. I just had to hope that I'd done the *barre* work and the arms well enough to make up for the steps.

After the *révérence*, Miss Coralie said she was going to tell us who she'd chosen to do the test. Everyone went to the front, but Jasmine and I stayed near the back of the group. Rose didn't even bother to listen at all. She just wandered over to the *barre* and put her right leg up on it. Miss Coralie didn't seem to mind. It was the end of the lesson, after all.

My heart was beating so hard it was making my top half go quivery. *Please let it be me... Please let it be me... Please let it be me...*

"Now, some of you might be disappointed not to be picked but, as you know, the more advanced you are at ballet, the harder it becomes, and I never let anyone take a test unless I'm very sure that they'll do well."

Everyone nodded and waited. My heart was thumping.

"There's going to be an extra class on Fridays

for those people doing the test, because once a week won't be enough..."

I stood as still as a statue waiting to hear who'd been chosen. But Jasmine was nudging me and jerking her head. She wanted me to look over at the *barre*. When I saw what Rose had done, I nearly gasped out loud. She was facing the *barre* standing on her left leg with the foot turned out. She'd slid her right ankle so far along the *barre* that she was almost in a kind of sideways split. Even Tamsyn Waters wouldn't be able to do that. It was amazing.

"So these are the people who will be doing the test this term..."

My eyes shot back to Miss Coralie.

"...and if you're not on the list, it simply means that you'll be doing it next time or whenever you're ready for it. It *doesn't* mean you're no good at ballet, or anything like that, because you're *all* good in this class."

She gave us a quick smile, then her eyes went

down to her piece of paper and my eyes went down to the floor.

"Lottie Carroll, Immy Pearson..." I saw them clutch each other and do a little jump of happiness. "...Tamsyn Waters, Sophie James, Isobel Brooks and Jasmine Ayed."

The floor seemed to have gotten all blurry. I didn't feel like looking up. Not ever again. Jasmine put her arm around my shoulder. I knew she was only being kind, but I felt like pushing her away because I didn't want her to touch me. My throat was hurting and I was scared that tears were going to come into my eyes. If only I could run away and find a dark little place where I could cry and cry and nobody would know.

Inside my head, a voice was saying: *It's all Rose's fault. She made you mess up.*

But then I suddenly realized something.

Miss Coralie had read the names off a list. That meant she'd already decided who was going to do the test before the lesson had even started. So I couldn't blame it on Rose. It was just me. I wasn't good enough. I just wasn't good enough.

4 Balancing Tears

"Guess what I've made? Tuna pasta!" said Mom.

She was using her bright, sparkly voice, the one she'd been using ever since Jasmine and I had gotten into the car and I'd told her I wasn't taking the test.

"Never mind," she'd said. "Miss Coralie knows best."

After that, I'd sunk down into the front seat and not said a single word because I felt too awful. It didn't matter though because Mom was doing enough talking for about ten people.

"Do you like tuna pasta, Jasmine?" she said,

lifting her chin so that her eyes could look in the rearview mirror.

"Yes," said Jasmine in a quiet voice. *She'd* been using her quiet voice ever since we'd left class.

"We're just going to pick up Stevie from Mark Mason's..."

That made me talk. "Oh, no! Mom, you said you weren't picking up Stevie till later!"

"Well, Mark's mom and dad have got to go out and they want to make sure Mark's ready for bed before the babysitter arrives, so I said we'd pick Stevie up early."

"Oh, Mom! He'll only pester me and Jasmine."

"No, he won't because I won't let him," said Mom, still in her bright voice. Then she suddenly sounded less bright. "Let's put some music on, okay?"

I think she was tired of talking. She was probably fed up with me, too. But I couldn't help being in such a rotten mood. This was the worst day of my life, and now it was even worse because I was going to have to put up with my little brother hanging around Jasmine and me.

I sighed a great big silent sigh that made my shoulders go up and back down again, then I slumped even lower into my seat. It was going to be horrible with Jasmine in a different class and me stuck with Rose Bedford and her grasshopper jumps and silly grunting noises. If it hadn't been for her, I would have done the step sequence much better, and then I might...

But I couldn't blame Rose, could I? All I could do was sit there with a big lump in my throat, listening to Mom's CD.

No one said another word till we got to Mark Mason's.

"You two stay here. I won't be a minute."

As soon as Mom had gotten out of the car,

Jasmine leaned forward. "Hey, Poppy, Miss Coralie might change her mind, you know... If you practice like crazy and I help you with the steps... And we could tell her that it was Rose messing you up..."

"But it wasn't just because of Rose..."

"Yes it was! You're normally *much* better than you were today."

"I wish she'd never joined our class. She made me do everything wrong."

"I know. It's not fair, is it? Does she act like that at school, too?"

"She's always playing with the boys. And she gets into trouble with the teachers all the time. I don't know why she's coming to ballet."

"Maybe her mom *made* her."

I nodded miserably.

"But if you really *really* practice the sequence like crazy and next week we tell Miss Coralie that you couldn't concentrate because of Rose..."

"I'm not sure..."

At that moment, my little brother yanked open the back door and got into the car.

"Hey, Mark's got a baseball cap with a light on it and he can even read in the dark, only it wasn't dark so we couldn't test it."

I didn't say anything. I didn't even turn around. My throat was hurting again. I just wanted to get home and go to my room and talk to Jasmine. I was glad she thought it was Rose's fault though, and not mine. That made me feel a little better.

"So you had a good time then, Stevie?" Mom laughed, buckling her seat belt.

"Yeah, wicked good!"

I don't know if Stevie suddenly realized that I was being quiet, but he leaned forward and peered at my face. "Why is Poppy crying, Mom?"

I stayed very still and tried really hard not to let any tears fall but it didn't work, so then my throat hurt from trying not to make any crying noises.

"Seat belt, Stevie. Now!" said Mom.

Stevie made Jasmine play thumb war with him for the rest of the way home, so I didn't have to say anything, thank goodness. I could feel Mom glancing sideways at me though. I managed to blink my tears away when she wasn't looking and then I concentrated hard on what Jasmine had said. Maybe she was right. Perhaps Miss Coralie *would* change her mind.

When we got home, Jasmine and I went straight to my room.

"I don't know what Papa's going to say," said Jasmine.

"Your *dad*?"

She nodded. "You know he hates ballet."

"Yes, but he lets you do it, doesn't he?"

"He doesn't mind at the moment, because he's no idea how much practice I do and how much I love it."

"Will he be mad that you're taking the test?"

"He might not let me do the extra lessons – then *I* won't be able to take the test either."

"Oh no!" I felt so sorry for Jasmine. "Couldn't you ask your mom not to tell him?"

Jasmine's eyes got huge as she shook her head.

I knew as soon as I said it that it was a silly idea. Jasmine's dad's scary strict. Jasmine's told me that she's only allowed to take ballet until she's eleven and then her dad wants her to concentrate on school work and the piano.

"You won't be eleven for a long time, Jasmine. So your dad won't mind."

She sighed a big sigh. "I'll have to make sure he doesn't realize how much ballet practice I'm doing. Otherwise, he'll only tell me that I'm neglecting my school work and how unnatural it is to do all that stretching and turning out and everything."

"It's better than turning *in*." I knew I was sounding snippy, but I couldn't help it. I'd remembered Rose again. "I felt kind of sorry for Rose Bedford at first, but I don't now. I wish Miss Coralie had made her stand next to someone who was good at steps. Then it wouldn't have mattered if she'd kept pestering them."

"Never mind her. Let's try the new steps," said Jasmine, jumping up.

But before you could say *sequence*, my door was pushed open and Stevie stood there looking guilty. "Mom says everything's ready to eat."

"Have you been listening outside my bedroom door, Stevie?"

"I only heard a little about Rose Bedford. What did she do?"

"Nothing," I said. But Jasmine had spoken at the same time.

"She made Poppy goof up and now Poppy can't take the test."

Stevie wasn't even listening. "Rose is so cool!"

Jasmine gave him a puzzled look. "What do you mean?"

I said nastily, "Stevie thinks anyone who plays with Archie Cook is cool."

"Who's Archie Cook?"

"Only the best soccer player in the whole school!" said Stevie. "He lets me join in sometimes. He says I'm not bad for my age."

"Come on, everyone. It'll get cold!" Mom called from downstairs.

The moment my brother had raced off, Jasmine put her arm around me. "We'll work on the new sequence after dinner, okay?"

"Okay, but I don't think it'll make any difference," I said in a glum voice.

"Yes, it will!" said Jasmine. Then she stuck her thumb up in the air. "Come on!" I put my thumb against hers, closed my eyes and made my silent wish.

Please let Miss Coralie change her mind next week.

5 Is It All a Trick?

The next morning at school was fun because in English class we were listening to music to help us with creative writing. Miss Morrison played my very favorite piece of music in the whole world – *Waltz of the Flowers* from *The Nutcracker Suite*. I was the last one to go out to play after the lesson because I wanted to finish what I was writing. I'd just come out to the playground, when I saw Rose Bedford with Tom Priest and Archie Cook.

It gave me a shock when Rose started talking to me as though we were best friends. "Hi. I've been waiting for you. I thought you'd gotten in trouble and were being kept in."

Tom Priest was grinning in a horrible way. "Do you take ballet?" he said to me.

I tried to be cool. "Yeah. So?"

Archie Cook put his arms up into fifth position – at least, what *he* thought fifth position was – and started turning around on tiptoe like one of those little ballet dancers in a music box.

I didn't say anything, just started to walk away.

"They're being silly. Ignore them," said Rose.

I kept walking because I didn't want to talk to Rose.

But she was following me. "Were you upset that you weren't chosen for the test?" she asked.

I felt like turning around and snapping: *It's all your fault, you know!* But I didn't dare, so I just shook my head and walked faster. I could see my friends, Mia and Alice, on the other side of the playground.

Rose was talking again. "I'm giving up the minute the lessons are over. I don't like it."

That made me turn around. "Why are you doing it then?"

"My mom's making me because my grandmother gave it to me for my birthday."

"What do you mean?"

"My present was ballet lessons, even though she knew I'd absolutely hate it."

"Why did she give you ballet lessons if she knew that you don't like ballet?"

"I think she wants me to stop being a tomboy and start wearing skirts and things like that."

I couldn't imagine Rose ever wearing a skirt, even if she did ballet for a hundred years.

"So you're definitely giving it up?" I knew it was horrible of me, but I wanted to be sure I wasn't going to have to put up with her for any longer than I had to.

"Yeah." She suddenly did one of the jumps where you have to beat your feet in the air. "Is this right?"

It wasn't, but I nodded anyway. Then I turned, because Mia and Alice were waving to tell me to come over.

Rose grabbed my arm. "Can you show me how to do it right, Poppy?"

I didn't really want to, but I thought that maybe, if I just showed her quickly, she'd leave me alone.

"You start like this, okay?" She copied my third position surprisingly well. "Then you bend your knees out to the side…"

A big whooping noise from the other side of the playground made Rose and me turn around at exactly the same moment.

Archie and Tom were by the drinking fountain pointing at me, and laughing.

"Shut up, you two!" called Rose. But, when she turned back, I saw that she was grinning.

"Okay, what do you do next?"

I suddenly realized I'd still got my legs bent in a *plié*, which must have looked totally stupid. A terrible thought came into my head. *I bet Rose tricked me into showing her the beats just so her friends could make fun of me.*

At that moment, I hated Rose Bedford. I really did.

6 Making the Air Swirl

On Saturday afternoon I went to Jasmine's house. Her dad was out. I was glad he wasn't there, because it's not just ballet he's strict about, it's things like playing with friends and watching television.

Jasmine's mom's not half as strict. I think she guessed that Jasmine and I would be practicing ballet up in Jasmine's room, but she just said, "I'm sorry about the test, Poppy." I liked the way Jasmine's mom sounded, all gentle. She's got a great accent because she's French.

As soon as we were on our own, I asked Jasmine if her dad minded the extra class.

"He's sort of annoyed about it, but I'm allowed to do it, thank goodness."

"That's super great, Jazz! Did you start the test dance?"

Her eyes sparkled. "Yes! That's why I asked Maman if you could come around. You see, I thought I could teach you the part we learned so you'll know it perfectly when Miss Coralie starts teaching the whole class on Tuesday. Then she'll definitely change her mind about the test!"

Jasmine's bedroom is much bigger than mine, but we made it even larger by clearing everything off the floor and putting her beanbag on the bed. We changed into our ballet things and did a warm-up so we wouldn't strain any muscles. Then we spent forever making sure I could do every single step of the dance perfectly.

"Right," said Jasmine. "Now for the sequence."

So then we worked on *that* too. But we didn't just go through it normally. We added a few extra parts to make it more interesting.

"Let's put it to music!" Jasmine suddenly said.

"Yesss! *Waltz of the Flowers!*"

We had to change the timing but it was great fun.

"I know it's a funny thing to say, but the air in this room feels different, doesn't it? As though we've made it swirl around because we've been dancing so much." I felt stupid saying it, but it was the way I felt.

Jasmine nodded and danced her fingers through the air as though she was testing it out. Then she stopped and said, "Let's ask Maman to come and watch."

At that moment, there was a knock at the door.

"Great, she's here!" said Jasmine, pulling open the door. "Maman, do you want..."

It wasn't Jasmine's mom, though. It was her

dad. A big smile covered his whole face. But when he saw that I was there, and that both of us were wearing our ballet leotards, the smile started to slide away.

"Hello, Papa!" said Jasmine, giving him a hug.

"Hello, Doctor Ayed," I said. Only my voice didn't come out properly because I was nervous, so it sounded like: "ElloDocAy".

"And what are you two doing?"

"Just...dancing..." said Jasmine. She sounded as nervous as *I* felt.

It must feel really strange to be scared of your dad, like Jasmine is. I'm glad I'm not afraid of mine.

"I can see that. But why, exactly?"

"Just making up a dance for fun, that's all."

Doctor Ayed frowned as though Jasmine had said something in a foreign language. "Hm..." Then he gave her what I call a *thin lips* smile. It's the sort of smile that grown-ups give you when they've got something to say that you probably don't want to hear but they're saving it up for later. "I see."

When he'd gone, the air stopped swirling around and stayed very still. So we sat on Jasmine's bed and I told her about Rose.

"I could tell she only got me to show her the jumps to make the boys laugh, Jazz."

"That was mean of her."

"I know. But I got her back, because when she tried to sit at my table at lunch I made sure there wasn't a seat anywhere near."

"Good. That showed *her*!"

"I know. And the next day she started talking to me in the playground, but Tom and Archie were with her so I didn't even answer. I think she finally gets it that I don't want to be friends, because today she didn't come anywhere near me."

"At least that means she'll definitely leave you alone at ballet next week."

I couldn't help feeling a little thrill of

excitement. But it only lasted for about a second, then my body went all limp like a wet towel. "It won't make any difference."

"Yes, it will!" said Jasmine, linking her arm with mine. "We're going to get Miss Coralie to change her mind, and that's that!"

"Do you really *really* think she might?"

"I really *really* do."

And this time I got a little tickle of excitement that didn't turn into a wet-towel feeling, but grew into a lovely big burst of sunshiny hope.

7 Trapped in the Circle

On Tuesday, I got more and more excited as the day went on. I'm always like this on Tuesdays, because I have ballet after school. I wish I could have ballet after school every single day. But *this* Tuesday was especially important. I had named it Last-Chance Tuesday.

At morning recess I rushed outside with Mia and Alice, but stopped when I heard Rose's voice behind me.

"Hey, Poppy…"

"What?" I asked, turning.

I got quite a shock. She was standing very

straight with her hair scraped back and not a tangle in sight. On her face was a proud grin.

"Thought I'd get myself all ready today so I won't be late! Look!" She spun around and I saw that she'd even twisted her ponytail into a bun and pinned it in place.

I didn't know what to say. The trouble was, if I acted nice and friendly, Rose would only start talking in the middle of ballet, and it would be absolutely terrible if she made me mess up again. So I just said, "Oh," and hoped she'd go away.

But she didn't. And to make everything super bad, a group of grinning boys suddenly appeared. They made a circle around us and I felt uncomfortable standing in the middle with Rose.

"Ro's getting girlie!" chanted Tom and Archie. "Ro's getting girlie!"

"I am *not*!" shouted Rose, sticking her neck out and nearly spitting, she was so angry. "Get lost!"

But they didn't.

I really wanted to escape and leave Rose, but something was stopping me. It was funny, but Rose with a neat bun seemed like a different girl from tomboy Rose. And I would have felt horrible leaving this new Rose with all those nasty boys, even though the boys were her friends.

"Talking to your little ballet friend?" asked Alex in a high-pitched voice.

"With your little bunny-bun-bun!" said Tom.

The other boys just laughed and started going around on tiptoe with bent legs and high arms, because that's the only ballet step they knew.

"Rosie Posie does ballet! Rosie Posie's getting girlie!" they all chanted.

"I am *not*! And don't call me that!" yelled Rose.

That only made them chant louder. "Rosie Posie! Rosie Posie!"

I could tell she was getting really furious, staring at the boys as though she would explode with anger. Then she suddenly reached up to her hair and started tugging. One or two hairpins fell to the ground. Next she ripped the rubber band off her ponytail. It must have really hurt her to yank it off that way. She shook her head hard a few times, and her hair fell around her shoulders, so she was back to normal.

The boys stopped circling us and stared at her.

She stared right back, with black eyes flashing in an angry white face, and spoke in kind of a snarl, "Did someone turn off the music?"

Then she punched Tom on the arm and, while he was clutching it, pushed past him and ran away laughing.

"I'll get you back, Ro! You wait!"

Tom raced after Rose and I was left standing there.

Archie Cook pointed at my face and started a new chant. "Poppy is pathetic!" Then the others joined in. "Poppy is pathetic! Poppy is pathetic!"

"I am *not*!" I said, trying to sound strong and tough like Rose had. But it didn't work.

A boy called Dillon started sneering. "Why d'you do ballet then?"

"Yeah, why d'you do it?" said Archie, laughing.

I took a deep breath to try and make my voice come out louder. "I'm not the only one," I said.

"Hey, Ro's told me what the teacher's called," said Dillon, grinning around at the others. "Miss Coralie!"

Archie started pointing his toes in that stupid ballet imitation and saying, "Ooh-hoo, look at me, Miss Coralie!"

I could feel my heart beating near my throat. That probably meant that I was going to cry in a minute, so I knew I had to get away *now*. If only Mia and Alice would come over and save me. I could see them talking to the teacher in the far corner of the playground. She was smiling and nodding at them.

Please look over in this direction. Please look over in this direction.

But they didn't.

Archie started jumping from foot to foot, pointing his toes. He looked really stupid. I couldn't bear it for a second longer. I'd just have to act like Rose for once. That was the only way I was ever going to get away. Before I could change my mind, I gave Archie a big shove on the chest and called out some words that I'd heard once on television. "Shut up, dirt bag!"

I was shocked when he lost his balance and fell over. "Owwww! You've broken my wrist!" he screamed.

The boys all got quiet and one of them crouched down beside Archie. "You all right?"

Archie just clutched his wrist tightly and made little grunting noises as he stared at it with his face all screwed up. I wished I could go back in time and undo my big shove.

"What's going on here!" Mrs. Appleton was hurrying over. She looked furious. Now I felt as though someone was trying to squeeze the air out of me.

"Poppy pushed Archie down," said Dillon, giving me a mean look.

"Sorry," I said. But my mouth was suddenly dry and my *sorry* came out as a whisper.

Mrs. Appleton bent down beside Archie and spoke in a soothing voice. "Just try moving it very gently, dear. That's right. Does it hurt when you do that?"

"Ouch!" yelped Archie. "I'm dying!"

Mrs. Appleton nodded. "Come on, let's get you on your feet... At least it's not broken."

"My back hurts too," Archie whined. Then he gave me a mean scowl. "And my chest..."

Mrs. Appleton suddenly turned to look at me. "What do you think you're doing Poppy? This isn't the way to behave! Imagine what it'd be like if Miss Cherry got upset with me and decided to push me over! That wouldn't be right, would it?"

I shook my head and tried to think of something to say that would show Mrs. Appleton I wasn't completely nasty. "Ah, well... you see...the thing is...Archie said ballet was stupid..."

"Well, I'm sorry, Poppy, but I'm afraid that is no excuse for hitting him. He's hurt his wrist and has probably got a bruise on his, er... lower back."

"It really hurts..." said Archie, clutching his bottom and screwing up his face.

Mrs. Appleton put her arm around his shoulder, told him gently that his wrist definitely wasn't broken, then said sternly to me, "What do you say to Archie?"

I caught a glimpse of Stevie near the fence, watching all that was going on.

"Sorry," I whispered for the second time, with a face like a tomato.

"I should think so! Don't do it again, do you hear me? That kind of behavior is not acceptable at this school!" She patted Archie's shoulder and added, "You can go now Poppy."

I didn't look at anyone. Just ran to Mia and Alice as fast as my shaky legs would take me.

None of the teachers gave me any accusing looks during lunch, so I made myself stop thinking about Archie Cook and his disgusting friends and concentrated on ballet instead. It was at the afternoon recess that my big jitters started. I decided to go to the restroom and practice the step sequence from the last lesson. I couldn't wait to show Miss Coralie that I could already do it perfectly before she even started to polish up what we'd learned last week.

The first thing I did when I got into the restroom was hold on to one of the sinks and do a *plié*. I like pretending the sink is a *barre* because it's exactly the right height. I sung the *plié* music very softly and did one facing the other way to make it even.

I was just straightening my legs when I thought I heard a little noise coming from one of the stalls. Uh-oh. Someone else was in the restroom, too. That meant someone must have heard me singing, so I decided to go to the bathroom myself. Then by the time I came out whoever it was would have gone and they wouldn't know it had been me singing. It was too bad I couldn't go into the classroom to dance, but we're not allowed inside during recess unless it's raining.

When I heard one of the toilets flushing, I thought *Good, they're going at last!* I counted to twenty, then flushed my own toilet and went back into the restroom. No one was there. Thank goodness.

I went through the step sequence four times, then I did the dance. I kept counting all the time, sometimes in my head, sometimes out loud. It helped me get it right. The noise of the end-of-recess bell made me jump because I'd been so wrapped up in my own little ballet world – my favorite place to be.

Just before I left the restroom, I said my little prayer for the sixty-sixth-millionth time... Only this time I said it out loud to make it work better.

"Please let Miss Coralie change her mind about me taking the test."

8 Goose Bumps

After school, Mom came to collect me and Stevie. She was standing at the gate, as usual, chatting to Mark Mason's mom, so I hung around with Mia, waiting impatiently for her to finish. I didn't want to be even ten seconds late for ballet. I wanted to make sure I had enough time to run through the sequence with Jasmine before the class started.

But I got a shock because when I looked again, Mom wasn't talking to Mrs. Mason any more. She was talking with Mrs. Appleton. And looking very serious. My heart sank and I felt myself tense. They had to be talking about me and

Archie. Mom was going to be really upset. I could just imagine her lecturing me all the way home. That was the problem with adults. They were the only ones who were allowed to talk when they were lecturing you. And if you dared interrupt they said you were being rude. I'd just have to make sure I said the word *bullying* right at the very beginning, because *that* would make her listen. Once I'd gotten her to listen, I'd explain about how Archie and his friends had been picking on me.

"I've got to go. Bye, Mia."

"Come on, Stevie. We're going," Mom called when she saw me walking across to her.

"Bye, Poppy! See you tomorrow!"

Mia was so lucky. She didn't have to worry about getting lectured or having her whole life ruined because of not being chosen for a ballet test.

The moment we got in the car, Stevie started telling Mom about soccer.

"You should have seen me, Mom, I was wicked good! Mr. Palmer said I did really excellent footwork. When we got back to the classroom, he gave me this sticker! Look! It says I'm a star! See!"

Stevie was leaning forward, tapping Mom on the shoulder.

"Sit down, Stevie, and put your seat belt on. I'll look when we get home."

Uh-oh! Mom didn't sound very happy, and I could easily guess why.

Stevie didn't seem to notice. He was too full of the goal he'd scored. "Mr. Palmer's written 'soccer' on the sticker, Mom. Now it says *I'm a soccer star!* Great, isn't it!"

Mom's voice reminded me of a pair of nail clippers. "Yes, great, Stevie. Is your seat belt fastened?"

"He said I was a sure bet for the varsity next year. What *is* a sure bet?"

No answer. I could see the side of Mom's face

from where I was sitting. It looked as though the bones were moving in her jaw. She was definitely thinking very cranky thoughts.

I was dreading getting home. Half of me wanted to get the lecture over with right here and now, but the other half thought that if I kept quiet Mom might just forget about it.

The moment we got home, Stevie kicked off his shoes and rushed off to watch cartoons, and I raced off to do my hair and get my ballet things ready. I was halfway up the stairs when Mom's voice stopped me.

"I want a word with you, young lady." Goose bumps came up under my school sweatshirt. "Come into the kitchen."

I shot back down as fast as possible, because I was so anxious about ballet. I couldn't be late on this most important day in the world, and the traffic was always really bad if we were even a little late.

"I know what you're going to say, Mom, and it wasn't my fault. Honestly. I promise. It was Archie big bully Cook and his friends saying nasty stuff about ballet..."

"Hold it right there, Poppy!"

Another coating of goose bumps sprang up all over me.

Mom put her hands on her hips. "Mrs. Appleton has told me the whole story, Poppy. You pushed Archie over. Hard. And he hurt himself! I cannot believe that a daughter of mine did that. I don't know what Dad'll say..."

"But..."

"Don't interrupt! It's all too easy to blame the boys, these days. But this time, Poppy, *you* were the bully!"

"I wasn't! It's not fair!"

"Which part isn't fair? Did you push Archie Cook over or not?"

"Y...yes...but it was because he was making fun of me." I knew my voice was getting louder but I couldn't help it. "And they made a circle around me and I couldn't get out..."

Mom pressed her hands together and put them in front of her lips, frowning.

"Made a circle?"

I thought that I was making her understand, at last. But then I suddenly caught sight of the clock and my whole body stiffened. "Oh, no! I'm going to be late for ballet. We've got to go right now or I'll get killed! I'll tell you in the car, okay?"

There was no time for another word. I just raced out the door. Unfortunately, it slammed behind me.

"Come back here!" Mom sounded *really* angry now.

"*Please* can I tell you about it in the car?" I said, poking my head around the kitchen door and trying to sound sensible and grown-up, even though I felt like screaming.

"No, you can't, because you're not going to ballet."

The blood seemed to drain out of my face and down my neck and my body until I was completely wobbly and weak. "What...?"

"Come in and close the door," Mom went on in her icy voice. "I haven't finished talking about what happened today, and you do *not* go racing off when I'm right in the middle of talking to you."

I stood with my head hanging down. This really was the worst moment of my life.

"Can I have a sandwich, Mom?"

Stevie had come sliding into the kitchen, which he always does when he's only got socks on his feet. Mom doesn't usually mind, but today she was in too much of a bad mood to put up with it.

"I'll bring you one in a minute. I'm talking to Poppy."

Stevie stopped sliding and stood with his legs wide apart. He could tell something was wrong. "What are you talking about?"

I was about to tell him to mind his own business when he suddenly answered his own question. "I bet it's Archie Cook."

I looked up then. Mom was frowning. "What do you know about that?"

"I heard Mrs. Appleton telling you that Archie hurt his wrist..." Stevie was slowly going down into a sort of sideways splits as his feet were sliding further apart. So the next part of what he said came out as grunts. "Only...he...never did...hurt...it..."

Mom marched over to Stevie and pulled him into a normal standing position. Then she tilted his chin to make him look at her. "Stand still and tell me what you're talking about."

Stevie did as he was told. "I just saw Archie laughing behind Mrs. Appleton's back, that's all."

"Laughing?"

"Yeah, when Poppy was getting in trouble."

My eyes widened. I wanted Stevie to keep

going, but I could tell he was getting hungry because his eyes kept darting over to the refrigerator.

"And how do you know that Archie hadn't hurt his wrist?" asked Mom.

"Because he was waving it around, showing off and making faces behind Mrs. Appleton's back when she was talking to Poppy. Then, the moment she turned around he pretended it was hurting again."

Now Mom's eyes were widening. They looked like big buttons. She didn't seem to be able to speak for a few seconds, but then it was as though someone had slapped her on the back and made the words come shooting out. "Go on then, Poppy, get your stuff, quick. We'll talk in the car."

I could have hugged Stevie, but there was no time. I couldn't waste a single second. I *had* to get to ballet on time.

9 Last Chance

"Calm down, honey!"

"I can't calm down. I'm worried."

All my wishing had meant nothing because here we were, stuck in a huge line of traffic, creeping along.

I yanked my leotard and tights out of my bag. "I'm going to get changed right now, Mom."

"People might see your underpants," said Stevie, grinning.

"Don't be silly, Stevie. Just calm down, Poppy. I'll come in and explain to Miss Coralie..."

"No. Parents don't come in. Not ever, Mom. You can't."

I wriggled out of my school skirt and managed to get my tights on without undoing the seat belt for more than ten seconds.

"It'd be great if we had a police siren, wouldn't it?" said Stevie. Then he made the noise of a siren until I'd got my leotard on.

"Oh, be quiet, Stevie. I can't drive with all that noise." I felt a little better because I only had my hair to fix, but my heart was still beating faster than usual because we were going so slowly.

Mom was making frustrated noises and craning her neck out of the car window. "This doesn't look too good."

"What? What?" I felt like crying. I'd just spotted the clock on the dash and it said twenty-five past four. The class started at half past.

"Look, Poppy, there's nothing we can do about it, so stop working yourself up."

But I couldn't stop. I *was* worked up. And I was frantically searching through my bag, looking for my hairband. It wasn't there.

"Oh, no! I haven't got my hairband! What am I going to do?" And then I *did* burst into tears.

The clock said twenty-eight minutes past four and our car wasn't moving at all.

"Why doesn't the light turn green?" I asked Mom through my tears.

"I'm afraid it's changed already, honey," said Mom, sighing a big sigh. "There's just so much traffic. It's because we got a late start." She turned to give me a consoling smile. "Put your hair in a bun, Poppy. You've got plenty of hairpins, haven't you?"

I nodded miserably and started doing what she said.

"Look, we're moving!" said Stevie.

I sat up straight to look, but we only moved about two yards. And when I saw the clock I started going crazy, shouting and crying at the same time.

"It's half past! I'm going to be late for sure now! And everyone'll stare and I haven't even got a hairband and that'll make them stare harder... It's no good. I can't go. Let's go home."

"No, we really *are* moving now," said Stevie. "Look, it's turned green! Go on, Mom, get through it quick!"

And a few seconds later we were in High Street, but we were still only crawling along.

"Bet Poppy could run faster than this car's going!" said Stevie.

I unbuckled my seat belt. "Yes! Can I, Mom?"

"No, it's too far on your own. We'll be there in a minute."

"Oh, pleeeeeease, Mom. You can watch me all the way. I'll leave my bag in the car and just take my ballet shoes. *Pleeeeeease!*"

We'd stopped again and I think that's what

made Mom agree. "Go on, then. I'll see you at the end of the lesson. Bye, darling."

I shot out of the car and onto the sidewalk and ran harder than I've ever run before, feeling silly because I was wearing my ballet uniform with my school shoes.

When I got to the heavy door, I crashed against it and it opened so easily that I fell inside. It hurt but I got up and went running up the steps. By the time I was at the top, I was completely winded. I heard the *plié* music, so I knew I'd only missed one thing.

I quickly put on my ballet shoes and noticed that there was a big black mark on my tights. That must have happened when I'd fallen downstairs. I gulped and rubbed it but it smudged more, so I left it and threw my shoes in the changing room, then stood glued to the floor outside Room One...

A little voice inside my head said: *You can't go in looking like that, Poppy.* But another fierce little voice said: *Just go, Poppy!* Before I could change my mind, I pressed my thumbs together, then took a deep breath and pushed open the door.

I didn't look at anyone. Just said, "Sorry I'm late," in a squeaky voice and went over to Jasmine. Her eyes were full of questions as she edged closer to Immy Pearson to make room for me. I knew everyone was staring at me, so I couldn't say anything, and anyway, Miss Coralie wanted to get on with class.

"Battements tendus... Preparation...and..."

I caught sight of myself in one of the mirrors and wished I could disappear into thin air. I was a mess. My face was bright red. It was obvious I'd been crying and my bun was nearly falling out. Then there was that awful black smudge on my tights.

Miss Coralie was using her no-nonsense counting voice, moving along the line with her straightest back and sternest face. When she got to me, she lifted up my arm to a more correct position. "No hairband, Poppy?"

"We were in a big hurry," I whispered, trying to keep my turnout and my *pointe*.

"Hmm."

She moved on to Jasmine and then to Lottie, all the time counting in a louder voice than usual. My heart was still thudding from running so hard, but now it was thudding from nervousness too.

It wasn't till we were over halfway through the *barre* work that I felt normal again. I took a quick glance around and saw that no one was looking at me any more, thank goodness. Okay, from now on I was going to concentrate like crazy and not let anything put me off. Especially Rose Bedford.

I suddenly realized that I'd completely forgotten about Rose until now. She was on the *barre* on the opposite wall with her hair looking tangled and knotted again, her hairband pressing her eyebrows down and her big leotard in wrinkles all over her stomach. There was *something* different about her though, only I couldn't figure out what.

"And *one* and *close* and *second* and *close*, derrière and *close* and *second* and *close...*" said Miss Coralie, walking slowly around, watching everyone with her eagle eye. "And *one* and *two* and *use* your *heads*, don't *roll* your *feet* and *straigh*ten knees." The music came to an end, but Miss Coralie wanted to do the whole exercise again. "A lot of you are gripping the *barre* far too tightly," she said. "Take a step away, and we'll try it without holding on at all."

I glanced at Rose. She had already stepped away from the *barre* and had her arms ready and everything. It was really strange. She seemed to be trying so hard, considering she hated ballet. And that reminded me of how she'd put her hair in a neat bun at school, even though she must have known the boys would tease her about it. I didn't understand Rose. She was a mystery girl.

"Concentrate, Poppy," came Miss Coralie's voice, and I realized I'd slipped into a daydream.

You stupid thing, Poppy! I said to myself. Then I made a promise inside my head that from now on I would do my very best every single second of the rest of the lesson.

When it was the *ronds de jambe*, Miss Coralie actually tilted her head on one side and said, "Very good, Poppy."

I wanted to skip around the room shouting, "Yesssssssss!" But I made myself stay completely still as though I hadn't even heard her.

Then it was time for the center work.

"Right, let's have the same rows as last week, but all move forward one row, and the front row from last week go to the back."

"Excuse me, Miss Coralie?" It was Rose who had spoken. Everyone stared at her because it's so unusual to hear anyone's voice except Miss Coralie's in ballet lessons. "Can I change rows, please?"

Miss Coralie looked puzzled. "Change rows? Why?"

"Er...because I was wondering if I could go on the back row today."

"Why?"

"So that I can copy better, because there'll be more people in front of me to watch."

Everyone waited to see what Miss Coralie would say.

"It'll mess up the numbers if I put you in the back row, Rose..."

"I could swap with someone..."

A frown crossed Miss Coralie's face. She wasn't used to anyone arguing with her. "Just stay where you were last week, next to Poppy. Thank you, Rose."

So Rose stood next to me, but she didn't look very happy. It was no surprise, really. After all,

I hadn't exactly been friendly with her at school.

When we did the *port de bras*, Miss Coralie had to tell Rose to stop crowding Sophie, who was on the other side of her, and to stand a little closer to me. I started wondering whether I smelled bad or something then, because Rose wouldn't care about having to stand next to me all *that* much.

I got another "lovely" from Miss Coralie for my *port de bras*, which gave me the crazy *yessssssss!* feeling, but still I didn't let it show. Then my heart started pounding with excitement as I thought, *Just wait till you see how well I can do the step sequence, then!*

We did lots of beats after the *adage* and, during this part of the lesson, Miss Coralie had to tell Rose to move up again because she was nearly jumping on Sophie's toes. Next, we did the ordinary steps and I saw from the clock on the wall that there wasn't much time left. I wished we could hurry up and get on with the step sequence that I'd practiced. *And* the dance.

"Now," said Miss Coralie, "this week, for a change, we're not going to do any polishing work on last week's sequence. Instead, I'm going to teach you another brand new set of steps because I think we need more practice at learning new sequences."

My heart sank down to my ballet shoes, and Jasmine turned around and gave me a worried look. I very nearly blurted out, *Please can we do the one we did last week first?* but managed to stop myself just in time. Miss Coralie wouldn't have been at all pleased if I'd tried to interfere with what she'd planned, too. She was already annoyed because Rose had argued with her.

The sequence seemed even more complicated than last week's. While Miss Coralie was showing us all the steps, my eyes started to water from concentrating so hard on her feet, trying to remember when it should be left in front and when right, when to face the left corner and when to face the right.

"Mark it through, Rose," said Miss Coralie in a slightly puzzled voice.

And that's when I noticed that Rose was standing completely still, staring straight ahead as though she was in a trance. "It's okay, thanks," she said, politely.

But Miss Coralie obviously didn't find it very polite. From the look on her face, you'd think Rose had called her a big fat pig or something. Her voice came out louder than usual. "I'm not asking you, I'm *telling* you."

Rose didn't go at all red, even though lots of people were giving her funny looks. She just started doing as she was told.

A minute later, Miss Coralie clapped her hands sharply. I think Rose had put her in a bad mood. "Okay, let's try it a row at a time. Front row first."

I watched Jasmine carefully, my mind racing away trying to remember everything.

"Not a bad attempt, front row. Second row, please."

This was it. I took a deep breath and got ready to focus.

"And…"

I tried my very hardest, but it was nearly as bad as last week. I could have burst into tears, because everything was going wrong.

We spent about five more minutes trying to improve the sequence, then Miss Coralie said that there wasn't time to start learning the dance. "Never mind, girls, we'll start it next week. Let's do the curtsy to finish."

I wished I could sink down through the floor and go on sinking down and down in the dark and stay there forever. My last chance was gone now. Really, really gone.

10 Friends

After the curtsy, Jasmine raised her eyebrows at me. She meant: *Wait till everyone's gone so we can talk to Miss Coralie.*

I gave a little shake of my head.

"Why not?" she hissed.

I whispered right in her ear. "There's no point."

"But what about the dance...?"

I shook my head again because I was too sad to speak, and started walking away. Everyone else had gone out except Rose, who was dipping her foot into the rosin tray at the back of the room. If Miss Coralie saw her she'd be really mad because you're not supposed to touch the rosin. It's for the older girls to give their ballet shoes extra grip when they're standing on *pointe*.

"Excuse me, Miss Coralie," said Jasmine.

I got a shock because I knew she was going to say something about me and I was certain Miss Coralie wouldn't listen. She was wearing a big frown, working out a step with her hands.

"Yes, Jasmine?"

Jasmine was using her politest voice. "I was wondering if you could possibly watch Poppy doing the dance."

I felt myself going red.

"I haven't time, I'm afraid, Jasmine. I'm starting the next class in a second." She wasn't even paying attention.

I opened the door, wanting to get away before any embarrassing tears started dripping down my face.

Then something surprising happened. Rose suddenly rushed up to Miss Coralie and blurted out, "It was *my* fault that Poppy didn't do her best last week. You see, I messed her up by standing right next to her and asking her to help me."

I stared at Rose, open-mouthed. Miss Coralie stopped what she was doing and looked shocked.

"Her brother told me in the playground. He said that he'd been eavesdropping at Poppy's bedroom door and he'd heard her talking to Jasmine."

Now Miss Coralie looked bewildered. "What *are* you talking about, Rose?"

"I'm talking about how I've been trying to keep away from Poppy and not do anything to mess her up today, because of it being my fault last time." Rose suddenly turned around to face me. "I even did my hair in that bun at school to show you that I was going to act like a real ballet student... Only then the boys made me so mad that I had to pull it out."

Jasmine suddenly interrupted. "So *can* Poppy show you the dance, Miss Coralie? Please?"

Miss Coralie looked as though she didn't know what on earth was happening.

"You should *see* her!" Rose suddenly blurted out. "She's super good!"

Miss Coralie frowned. "What dance?"

"The one you've started teaching for the test," said Rose. "Go on, Poppy, show her."

I couldn't figure out how Rose knew that I'd learned the dance. Was she a mind-reader or something?

"You've learned the test dance?" asked Miss Coralie, looking as puzzled as I felt.

"Jasmine showed me," I said quietly.

"Go *on!*" said Rose, as though she was my mom. "Do it how you did it in the restroom."

"You...*saw* me?"

She was grinning. "Yeah, I was hiding in the

stall, watching through the crack where the hinges are! You looked like a real ballerina. Go on!"

Miss Coralie flapped her hand and looked a little irritated with Rose. Her eyes were on me. "Are you telling me that you've learned the test dance all the way through and that you know it thoroughly?"

I nodded.

She looked at her watch for a long moment, as if she was having trouble telling the time. Then she said, "All right... Just very quickly ..." She gave Mrs. Marsden a sharp nod and turned back to me. "I'll count you in, Poppy."

Mrs. Marsden played the introduction. The music gave me a shock because I'd never heard it before and I hadn't imagined it would be so beautiful. It made the room feel like a stage, full of lights that swayed and glittered.

"*One* and *two* and *three* and *four*..."

It was a wonderful feeling because there was

no need to concentrate on the counts any more now. In fact, I didn't need to concentrate on anything. The music did all the work. I just danced and danced...

As I held the last position, Rose started clapping and whooping. I hardly dared to look at Miss Coralie but, when I did, I saw that her eyes were bright and dark at the same time.

"Lovely, Poppy," she said slowly. "Lovely. I truly didn't know you had it in you!"

"So, can she take the test then?" asked Rose, dropping to her knees right in front of Miss Coralie and folding her hands as if she were about to pray.

Mrs. Marsden let out a giggle and I noticed the corners of Miss Coralie's mouth twitch. But then she suddenly looked worried and spoke quickly. "Did you mail the letter of application yet, Mrs. Marsden?"

Out of the corner of my eye, I saw Jasmine's shoulders go up and heard her gasp. She must have been thinking exactly the same thing as me. Now that Miss Coralie thought I was good enough, it would be absolutely terrible if it was too late.

Mrs. Marsden reached down into her handbag and pulled out a big envelope. At the same time, a piece of paper fluttered out and landed at my feet. I didn't look at it because I was watching Mrs. Marsden. She straightened up, waved the envelope in front of our noses, grinned and said, "You're in luck. I forgot to mail the envelope at lunchtime!"

"What a relief!" said Miss Coralie, taking the envelope from Mrs. Marsden and slitting it open with her finger. "I'll put your name down, Poppy."

"Oh, thank you!" I cried. At least, that's what I tried to say, but my mouth was all dry again, so it just came out in a squeak.

And then I looked down and saw what was written on the piece of paper that had fallen out of Mrs. Marsden's handbag. It was the list of names that Miss Coralie had read out last week – the girls who she'd chosen for the test. I reached down and picked it up and, as I handed it back to Mrs. Marsden, I read them very quickly...

Lottie Carroll
Immy Pearson
Tamsyn Waters
Sophie James?
Isobel Brooks
Jasmine Ayed
Poppy Vernon?

I managed to keep my gasp inside. So I *was* on the list. My name was one of the ones with a question mark. I'd tell Jasmine later. But, for now, I could only smile and smile as all my old sadness faded away and a whirlwind of happiness started spinning inside me. I *had* been good enough. Miss Coralie would have picked me if I hadn't messed up so badly in that one lesson.

Jasmine put her arm around me and said, "I knew you could do it, Poppy." Then Rose got up and surprised me by giving me a hug.

"And so did I!" she said loudly.

"What a lucky girl you are, Poppy," said Mrs. Marsden, "having two such good friends!"

It was funny, because only a few minutes ago Rose hadn't felt anything like a friend. But now she really did.

"Off you go then," said Miss Coralie, shooing us away with her hands. "I've got another class waiting, you know."

Five minutes later we were walking downstairs together.

"I've just realized something," said Rose.

"What?"

"We're all flowers, aren't we? Poppy, Rose and Jasmine!"

Jasmine and I looked at each other with laughing eyes. "Are you thinking what I'm thinking?" I asked her.

"*Waltz of the Flowers!*" we both said together.

Jasmine turned to Rose. "Do you want to be part of the dance we've made up to Poppy's most favorite piece of music in the whole world?"

"No, I'd only ruin it," said Rose. "I'm so rotten at ballet... But you can ask me over and I'll watch you two dance."

"Yeah, let's go and ask Mom right now!" I said.

"And you can tell her your excellent news!" said Jasmine, dropping her bag and sticking both thumbs up, she was so happy.

Without thinking I pressed my thumb against hers.

"Hey, what about me?" said Rose, yanking my school shoes out of my other hand and making me join thumbs with her. Then she pressed her other thumb against Jasmine's so we made a triple thumb-thumb.

My eyes met Jasmine's and we burst out laughing. Then Rose broke free and raced off down the spiral staircase crying "*Plie* away! One and two and three and four! " at the top of her voice.

Jasmine and I followed behind and, for once, I couldn't hear the splitching echoing sound that our footsteps were making, because we were laughing so hard.

The End *

* *

* *

Jasmine's
Lucky
Star

1 Turning Point

Hi! I'm Jasmine. And right now I'm feeling very excited because my best friends, Poppy and Rose, are coming for a sleepover. In a way, I wish it was just Poppy coming, so we could keep practicing our ballet piece. We're doing the choreography ourselves and it's important to make it really good because it's for the end-of-year ballet recital.

Poppy and I don't go to the same school, but we take ballet together every Tuesday and we go to each other's houses a lot. She'll be here in a minute, and Rose isn't coming till a little later, so that gives us time to work on the dance. But maybe "work" isn't the right word, because ballet is our very favorite thing in the whole world...

"Jasmeen!"

That's my mom calling me from downstairs. She's French, so she speaks with an accent. I bet I know what she wants.

"I've done it, Maman!" I called back. (I've always called her "Maman". It's the French for "Mom".)

"I can't talk through the door, Jasmeen!"

I went out onto the landing and leaned over the stair railing. "I've finished it all, I promise."

"Good girl. Papa will be pleased." She broke into a smile and I broke into a shiver. That's the effect my dad has on me. He's away at a doctors' conference at the moment, and I know it's horrible of me, but I like it when he's away. You see, he's very strict – stricter than any of my friends' dads. Even worse than that, he doesn't approve of ballet. He thinks there are much more important things that I should be doing, like homework. I also have a tutor once a week so that's even more homework. Then there's my piano practice that my teacher expects me to do five times a week for at least twenty minutes each time. It gets on my nerves. All I want to do is ballet!

When I'm eleven, Papa says that I'm going to a school called Mansons where the work's really hard. Rose's brother knows someone who goes there and he says you have to take tons of exams and pass them with very high grades and end up being a lawyer or a banker or a doctor or a big chief executive or something.

And that's the problem. I don't want to be any of those things. All I want to be is a ballerina. Papa doesn't know that and, believe me, I'd never *ever* dare tell him. If he knew, he'd go crazy and probably make me give up ballet lessons immediately. He wasn't very happy when I was getting ready for my ballet test and I had to have a few extra lessons. At the moment, I only have one lesson a week. He doesn't mind that because it doesn't interfere with my homework or the extra work that my tutor gives me, or my piano practice or anything. He doesn't realize how much time I spend practicing ballet up in my room.

The worst thing of all is that Papa says I've got to give up ballet when I leave grade school. I used to think that was ages and ages away and that he'd have changed his mind by then, but I'm ten now and I'm scared that time's running out.

Rose is always saying that one of these days she's going to tell my dad a thing or two. I haven't known Rose as long as I've known Poppy, so she's never actually met Papa. Poppy and I have both tried to explain that he's not the kind of dad that you go around "telling a thing or two" to, but Rose doesn't really get how strict he is.

"Poppy will be here in a few minutes, *chérie*," called Maman. "Is your room neat?"

I sighed. "Yes, my homework's done and my room's neat and clean."

"Oh, there she is now!" Maman turned at the sound of the doorbell.

"It's okay, I'll get it." I shot downstairs and got to the door just before Maman.

Poppy was standing on the doorstep with her bag, her hair already scraped back in a bun, her ballet hairband on and a big smile on her face. "Hi, Jasmine! Look!" She yanked the snaps on her denim jacket apart. "I'm ready! I've got my tights on under my jeans."

Then my mom came into view and Poppy turned pink. She often turns pink. She's got the kind of skin that shows it easily – very fair with freckles, to go with her amazing auburn hair.

"Hello, Poppy. Good to see you!" Behind her in the car, I could see Poppy's mom smiling and waving.

"I'll just check and see what time your mom wants to collect you tomorrow," said Maman, patting Poppy on the shoulder as she went past.

"As late as possible!" I called out, dragging Poppy inside. "Come on, let's go to my room."

As soon as we closed the bedroom door behind us, Poppy bounced on my bed, pulling off her backpack. "I'm so excited. We've got plenty of time, haven't we? I really want Miss Coralie to be totally impressed on Tuesday when she sees how hard we've worked. How much of the dance have you made up so far?"

I was getting changed, smoothing my tights and putting on my leotard. "The *whole* dance! It's because I love the music so much. I can't wait to show you."

Poppy jumped up. Her eyes were shining. "I think we chose the *best* music. I'm so glad we were all allowed to take the tape of our dance home."

"Which is your favorite part?"

"Probably the tinkly high part...or maybe the ending...or that shimmery sliding part..." Poppy lay back on my bed and started doing scissor legs. "It was incredible when Miss Coralie said that we could choreograph our own dances for the show, wasn't it? Thank goodness I've got you for my partner. You're so much better than me at figuring out which steps go together to make the best choreography." She drew her knees up and hugged them tight.

I was standing in front of my mirror, doing my hair, but Poppy's words took me back to Tuesday's lesson. When I looked at my reflection, all I could see was a picture of Miss Coralie's face, her eyes flashing around our silent group as she told us about the show.

"This is a ballet school with a reputation for a very high standard of dance, so I want to see some serious work going on. Then we'll have a professional, high-quality show that we can all be proud of."

I concentrated on pulling my ponytail tight, trying not to let a single hair move out of place as I looped the band, so there would be no trace of any bumps. But I was so used to doing this that my hands could manage it without any help from my brain. That meant my mind could wander where it wanted. I saw Miss Coralie's no-nonsense look again.

"The show is to be called 'Shades of Nature' and it's in three sections. The first one is for all the younger pupils. They are doing dances based on animals, birds and flowers. The older girls are going to be working in three groups, representing earth, fire and water..." The silence had been so deep at that moment that you could have heard a flower opening. I remember how Miss Coralie's eyes had moved slowly over us.

"Your class, and the one that comes before you on Tuesdays, will make up the middle section of the show. You will dance the sky, the

moon...the stars, the sun...or any kind of weather – snow, frost, mist..." Her hands had been floating in graceful movements as she'd given us the list, but then they'd suddenly stopped in midair for her next words. *"And I shall not be doing the choreography. YOU will!"* There'd been a huge gasp and murmur when she'd said that, like a sparkler crackling into life, but then dying down to a quieter crackling excitement when Miss Coralie went on to explain that we had to work in groups of two, three or four. *"I don't think you should form larger groups than this, because you'll need to get together to do extra practice between lessons..."*

The moment I'd heard the word *extra*, my heart had started racing. Just remembering it sent a shiver right through me now as I pushed my hairband into place. It turned out that Miss Coralie had only meant extra practice at home, not extra real rehearsals or anything, but my very first thought had been: *"Oh, no! Papa won't let me do any extra rehearsals. What if I'm not allowed in the show?"*

"What are you thinking about, Jazz?" Poppy's voice made me jump.

"Nothing much."

"Bet it was your dad."

She was standing just behind me now. I smiled at her in the mirror. "You're a good mind-reader, Poppy."

"You always wear that look when you're worrying about your dad. What's he done now?"

"Nothing. I was just imagining how terrible it would have been if there'd been extra rehearsals for the show and he'd said I wasn't allowed to go."

Poppy put her hands on her hips and heaved a big sigh, pretending to be exasperated with me. "Well there *aren't* any, so you don't have to worry, do you?"

I didn't reply, just went over to my tape recorder and started rewinding the tape.

"Is he coming to see you?"

I wasn't sure what Poppy meant. "Who?"

"Your dad. Is he coming to watch you in the show?"

My stomach was suddenly full of butterflies. "I hadn't even thought about that. I don't know... I suppose so..."

"Well that's good, isn't it?" said Poppy. "Because then he'll see how excellent you are and it might make him change his mind about the whole thing and say you're allowed to keep on taking ballet lessons, even after grade school!"

My heart nearly stopped when she said that. "But what if he thinks I'm totally awful instead and says I've got to stop ballet forever?"

"Don't be silly, Jazz. You're the best. We're the youngest in the class *and* only you and Tamsyn won honors in grade four. That proves it!"

I turned and looked at Poppy. Her eyes were shining and her hands were clasped together as though she'd just heard that she'd been accepted into the Royal Ballet. "This could be a very, very important moment in your life, Jazz. When did your dad last see you dancing on a stage?"

I thought back. It seemed a very long time ago. "Well, he couldn't come last year because he was away on business. And the year before that...oh, yes, he had to do an emergency operation... Erm...I think it must have been three years ago."

Poppy jumped up, grabbed one of my hands and squeezed it tight. "You were only little then. He's no idea how good you are *now*, Jazz. You'll give him a major shock!" Her eyes sparkled. "Just imagine, he'll be sitting in the audience expecting to see you come on in a little frilly tutu and start twirling around with your hands above your head, looking like you did the last time he saw you. Then he'll sit up straighter than straight and stare his head off, because you'll be so incredibly good he won't believe it!" Poppy suddenly gave me her most serious look and spoke in a slow, solemn voice. "So it's very important, Jazz, that you do your best-ever choreography and your very-best-ever dancing. It'll be more than just a dance. It'll be a...a turning point in your life. Your dad will realize he *can't* stop talent like yours and he's *got* to agree to let you be a ballerina forever!"

Goose bumps started to come up all over my arms. The nice, shivery, magical sort of goose bumps. Poppy was slowly beginning to smile. It was as though her happiness was spreading from her hands into mine. It might be possible. It just might. And if I *could* make it happen, it would be the best thing that had ever *ever* happened to me.

The moment I'd had that thought, every drop of happiness dissolved into thin air. "But Papa knows what level I am in ballet. He said,

'Well done,' loads of times when I got honors for the test."

"That's not the same," said Poppy firmly. "My parents both said well done when I got a prize for merit, but they don't have a clue what that means. They don't know how much progress I've made. They never get to see us really dance, do they?"

I sighed a long, slow sigh. "Do you really, really believe I could make him change his mind, Poppy?"

For answer, Poppy pressed her thumb against mine. It's our special good-luck signal. We call it a thumb-thumb. And this time I knew I was going to need luck more than ever.

2 Starshine

"What time's Rose coming?" asked Poppy, her hand on the back of my chair. She was using it as a *barre* to hold on to while she did some *pliés* to warm up.

"Oh, no! She'll be here in an hour," I said, looking at my watch.

The moment I'd spoken, I felt embarrassed. It sounded like I didn't want Rose here. When I'm embarrassed, I don't turn red like Poppy, I just feel all hot, because redness doesn't show up on my olive skin. My dad's Egyptian, so that's where I get my dark skin from.

"Let's start working on the dance, quick," said Poppy. "We need to do as much as possible before she gets here."

I felt better knowing that Poppy agreed with me about that. You see, Rose has only been doing ballet for a little while. She really hated it when she first started, and she doesn't exactly love it now, but at least she doesn't hate it any more. All the same, I *know* Rose, and so I said, "She'll get bored fast watching us, won't she?"

"Maybe she could pretend to be one of those critics from the newspaper who writes about ballets they've seen?" suggested Poppy doubtfully.

I tried to imagine Rose sitting down and writing about me and Poppy practicing. "I suppose she could tell us which parts are good and which are bad..."

"None of it will be bad," said Poppy. "*Will* it?" she added, giving me a pretend stern look to make sure I'd remembered about making this dance the best ever.

A little shiver went through me again. "Okay, let's get started." I went over to the tape recorder.

"Oh, wait a minute," said Poppy, rooting around in her backpack. "I made up a poem to go with the dance, and I was wondering if we could record it onto a cassette and play it to the audience before the music started..." She suddenly turned pink again. "I mean, only if you like the poem...I've called it 'Starshine'."

I took the piece of paper that she was holding out and started reading. I'm normally a fast reader, but the words of Poppy's poem made me slow down. "It's wonderful, Poppy! You're so smart. We'll show it to Miss Coralie on Tuesday!" Then I had an even better idea. "Why don't we call our dance *Starshine* too?"

Poppy smiled and sat up straight on the bed.

"Okay, show me what you've choreographed so far."

"Okay. I'll try to explain at the same time. We start in opposite corners at the back... If this is the stage and that's the audience, I'll be here and you'll be there..." I said, putting the music on, "...and we'll run forward on on our toes, and finish in this position, only you'll be facing this way. And this fast part goes like this..." I started doing the repeated sequence of *pas de bourrées* and *jetés* that I'd worked out, but it suddenly seemed too easy. I was sure I could make it better... "Actually we ought to have *sissonnes* and *echappés* in here as well...yeah, and we could do it in a round!" Poppy was looking a little puzzled, but I knew she understood all the French names of the steps, and she'd soon pick up how to do it, so I just kept going.

"This part will be me doing that *pas de bourrée* step I showed you near the beginning, and you'll be doing it on the other side, only with your arms in second…" I was imagining my dad in the audience. Oh, dear. It wasn't going to be good enough. "Maybe we could do some *fouettés* here…I know we've never learned them, but I think I can do them…and then suddenly go into an *arabesque* with arms like this."

The more I talked, the more Poppy's eyebrows began to draw together, until they were practically joined up she was wearing such a enormous frown.

"I'm not sure I'll be able to do all this, Jazz…"

"You'll be fine, Poppy, honestly. Look…" I showed her a short sequence of *temps levé*, *chassé, pas de bourrée*, into fourth, and *pirouette*. "See," I said, a little breathlessly, "and you could do it on the opposite leg to the opposite corner so we're mirroring each other…"

"Can you just slow down a little, Jazz…?"

The trouble was, I couldn't slow down. I had so many ideas in my head now and I kept wanting to change things to make the dance better and better. It had to be perfect, absolutely perfect. Then Papa would think I was talented, and he might let me keep studying ballet.

But suddenly a loud silence filled the room. Poppy had gone over to the tape recorder and pressed the stop button. Her shoulders were slumped and when she spoke her voice was barely more than a whisper. "I'll never pick it up like this, Jazz. I'm not as good as you..."

I put hand to my mouth, feeling terrible. I didn't know what had gotten into me. "Yes, you *are*. It's totally my fault." I gave her a hug. "I shouldn't keep changing it all the time."

Poppy collapsed onto the bed. "Why don't I just sit here watching, and you tell me when you're absolutely sure that you're not going to change it any more?"

"No, it's okay. I'm going right back to what I made up before. Come on, let's start at the very beginning, and this time I *promise* not to change anything."

So that's what we did and, about an hour later, Poppy had learned the whole dance. She'd written it all down too so she could practice at home.

"It's so cool, Jazz!" she kept on saying. "I can't wait to show Miss Coralie on Tuesday. I'm going to do so much practice that I'll be able to do it standing on my head by then!"

I tried to be happy too. I really did, but there was a little voice nagging away at me, telling me that the dance could still be better. *Should* be better. I sighed inside, but I didn't let it show on the outside, because Poppy would be completely miserable if I tried to start changing things again now. And, anyway, Rose would be here any minute.

"Hey, you guys!"

And there she was right on time, standing in the doorway wearing a pair of jeans that looked very old and faded and a little too big for her. I bet they used to belong to one of her brothers.

Rose has got three big brothers and she often wears hand-me-downs, as she calls them. She doesn't care at all. In fact, I don't think she'd care if she was wearing a pair of pajamas.

"Your mom let me in. I heard the music when I was in the hall. It sounds really great." She dropped her bag on the floor and pushed it into the corner with her foot. "Show me how it goes!"

I really did not feel like showing Rose our dance, because I knew it would only make me want to start changing things again. "We'll show you when we've finished it, okay?"

"Oh, come on, Jazz! I've been dying to see it. I can help you if you need any ideas."

Poppy gave me an anxious look and Rose burst out laughing. "I'm kidding! You should see the looks on your faces!"

Then we were all laughing.

"Okay, I'm ready!" Rose said, bouncing down on the bed and then sitting up perfectly straight. "Hit it!"

I still didn't feel like going through it again though. Poppy didn't look exactly thrilled either. All the same, she got into her starting position, so I went over to the tape recorder. But when I turned around, Rose was standing up with Poppy's poem in her hand. "Hey! Cool!" she breathed. "Where did you get this from?"

"Poppy made it up," I told her.

"Wow! You could have it at the beginning of your dance, you know! Then the audience would get what the dance was all about."

"That's what *we* thought," said Poppy, turning all pink again. "We're going to ask Miss..."

But Rose was reading out loud as though she was performing on television.

The sky is deep and dark.
The sky is dark and deep.
The world is still and silent.
Everyone's asleep...

As she read, the poem came to life. And by the time she'd finished, I'd had the most brilliant idea. "Why doesn't Rose stand on the stage at the very beginning of our dance and read the poem out loud to the audience!"

Poppy's eyes sparkled as she looked at Rose. "Yes, that would be perfect," she said, "because we'd all be in the dance then...in a way."

Rose shook her head slowly and broke into a big smile. "I just knew you couldn't do without me."

So, for the second time since she'd arrived, we were all laughing together.

3 Filling up the Music

The sleepover was perfect. First we all tried to squeeze into my bed, but it didn't really work because Rose kept wriggling all the time. So Poppy slept in my bed and Rose and I had sleeping-bag beds on the floor. Even then, we couldn't get to sleep because Rose kept complaining that her sleeping bag was too babyish. In the end I let her have my dark blue one, and I had the one covered in pink teddy bears.

The last thing I remember before I went to sleep was Rose telling jokes that she'd learned from her brothers. In the morning, she told us that she was right in the middle of one when she suddenly realized that Poppy and I were both fast asleep. At breakfast, we asked her to tell us the joke again, but she was too busy eating.

"I love croissants," she said, spitting crumbs of puff pastry out of her mouth by mistake. "Uh-oh. Sorry!"

Maman laughed. "Me too," she said. "They make me think of breakfast at home when I was a little girl."

Rose licked the end of her finger and pressed it onto a flake of croissant on her plate, then stuck it in her mouth, grinning at Maman. "Waste not, want not. That's what *my* mom's always saying."

Poppy smiled nervously because she's much shyer in front of people's parents than Rose is. I'm fine with anyone's parents. Except my own dad...

Rose dabbed every single little flake of

croissant from her finger into her mouth, one at a time. She seemed to take *forever*. The very second she'd finished, I asked Maman if we could leave the table.

"Yes, if you've all had enough. What are you going to do this morning?"

"Practice our dance," I said quickly.

Rose was not impressed. She pretended to go cross-eyed. "Are there any more croissants?"

Maman laughed. "I don't know where you put it all!"

So, while Rose had another croissant, Poppy and I went upstairs to practice. But from the moment we started dancing, my legs felt like lead because I'd gotten that feeling again. And this time it was too big to ignore. I just knew that there was more in the music than there was in our dance. And I also knew that I'd never be happy until I'd made it perfect.

Maybe if I made just a teeny change to start with. "Try this, Poppy..."

"Oh, no... Not again, Jazz! I was just getting good at it yesterday. Please don't say you want to change it."

"Only a little, honestly."

I tried to stop after the first change, but I couldn't because more and more ideas were tumbling out. *Sissonne en avant, sissonne en arrière, sissonne en avant, soubresaut, soubresaut,* and all the time arms changing position. When I finally looked up, Rose was standing beside Poppy. I hadn't even heard her come in.

"Isn't Poppy *in* this part then, Jazz?"

I felt guilty when she said that. And selfish too.

"It's okay," said Poppy quietly to Rose. "It's just that Jazz is trying to make it as perfect as possible for her dad."

"For her *dad*! Why? He doesn't even *like* ballet!"

I had to admit that it seemed weird when

Rose put it like that. But she didn't understand.

Poppy tried to explain. "You see, Jazz and I think that if her dad comes to watch the show and he sees how talented she is, he might let her keep studying ballet after all."

Rose rolled her eyes. "Huh! Very kind of him, I'm sure! You're already wonderful, Jazz. You shouldn't have to prove that to your dad, you know!"

I was starting to feel angry. The trouble was, in my heart I knew that Rose was right. But she didn't realize about Papa. He really *would* stop me taking lessons at the end of grade school unless I somehow managed to make him change his mind. I heaved a big sigh. I was sick of thinking about it all the time. Immediately, Rose shot across the room and hugged me, hard. "Don't worry, Jazz. Just wait till he gets back from his conference. I'm going to tell him a thing or two, you'll see!"

My heart did a backflip.

"You can't talk to him, Rose," said Poppy, looking anxious. "You'll make him angry."

"What time's he coming home?" asked Rose.

"Not till after you've gone," I quickly said (which was true).

"Maybe I'll leave him a note," said Rose, looking thoughtful. But, a second later, she'd broken into her usual grin. "Only kidding!"

Rose had to go home after lunch, so Poppy and I spent more time working on the dance.

"Miss Coralie won't believe her eyes, Jazz. She'll be really pleased with your choreography," said Poppy.

I pretended to agree, but still the little voice inside my head kept jabbing away at my brain. *It's not good enough. It's not good enough. It could be better. It could be better.*

Poppy's mom came to pick Poppy up just after that and, while our moms were talking, we did a quick thumb-thumb.

"Hope Miss Coralie lets Rose say the poem," whispered Poppy.

I nodded, but I wasn't thinking about that.

After they'd gone, I went back up to my room and got my bag ready for school the next day. Then I sat on the floor and listened to the *Starshine* music with my eyes closed. I went through the steps in my head, trying to picture myself with Poppy, performing our dance on the lovely big stage at the new Community Center Hall. I concentrated hard right up to the final position and then I imagined the clapping. When it finished I stayed perfectly still with my eyes closed, wondering why I felt so empty.

I got up slowly and rewound the tape. I didn't press play right away. Instead I stood at the window and looked at the sky. The bluey-gray was beginning to turn dark and smudged. I felt sure that what I could see was only the first layer of sky and that there would be more and more layers, each one a shade deeper than the last.

> *The sky is deep and dark.*
> *The sky is dark and deep.*
> *The world is still and silent.*
> *Everyone's asleep...*

Without taking my eyes off the sky, I felt behind me for the play button on the tape recorder and pressed it. As I stared into the distance, I imagined two glinting stars, weaving and crisscrossing, zipping and spinning. And every loop, every swirl and twirl left the finest trail of glittering silver dust behind it. My head was filled with the magic of the dance and I could see the steps I wanted, completely clearly now. I rushed to get my notebook so I could write them all down.

For the next few minutes, there was not a sound in my room. Yet, inside my head, the music was playing loudly and clearly.

I put the tape back on and danced the new steps through, imagining Poppy's part at the same time. At last, the dance had come alive. It all worked perfectly. I rewound the tape and tried it once more, but this time I heard something else above the sound of the music. It was Rose's words inside my head. They seemed to be mocking me.

"You're already brilliant, Jazz. You shouldn't have to prove that to your dad, you know."

"That's it!" I suddenly blurted out to the empty room. I could feel a kind of strength pushing its way out from my brain, right to my fingertips and the ends of my toes. I'd realized something important. I'd made the dance as good as I could make it. I'd done my very very best. I'd done it for Papa. So he could see me doing my very best. But it wasn't just for Papa. It was also for *me*.

I sat down on the bed feeling happy. Thank

goodness I'd decided to play through the music again. Thank goodness I'd managed to empty my mind of the old steps and let the music fill it up with the new ones. All I had to do now was to teach Poppy. She wasn't going to be very happy when I told her that I'd changed it again, and it would be much more difficult to learn this new version, but once she'd learned it, I felt sure she'd realize how much better it was.

I went straight down to Maman and asked her if it would be okay for Poppy to come over the next day after school. She hesitated at first, but when I explained how important it was, Maman said I could call and ask her.

"Hi, Poppy! Guess what!" I didn't wait for her to guess. "I've changed the dance. Only don't worry, it's…"

"Oh, Jazz… You shouldn't have! Your dad will be impressed with what we've done already…"

"No, that's just it, Poppy. I've changed it

because *I* wanted to make it better. I've done it for me."

Poppy didn't say anything. She obviously wasn't convinced. So I started talking really fast. "It's a trillion times better than it was and I just know you're going to love it when I show you it and Miss Coralie will be much more pleased than she would have been."

"But we won't be able to show her, because I won't have learned it!"

"That's what I'm calling about. Can you come to my house to practice tomorrow?"

I heard a big sigh. "Wait a second and I'll ask Mom."

I could hear Poppy and her mom talking and talking, and I could feel my spirits sinking at the same time because it sounded as though Poppy's mom had made other plans.

I was right. "Sorry, Jazz. Mom says I can't because her friend who's a hair stylist is coming. She's doing me and Stevie *and* Mom, so Mom won't be able to drive me over."

Maybe there was a glimmer of hope. "Well, I could come to your house instead."

"That's what I just said to Mom, but she said no. I asked if I could go to ballet early on Tuesday though, and she said that's fine."

That was something, at least. I'd just have to learn my new choreography until I knew it backward, then teach Poppy as much as possible before class. When I put the phone down I raced back upstairs to listen to the music again. I marked through the new steps, and suddenly I was imagining Papa in the audience. And then something hit me. What if Papa *wasn't* in the audience? What if he was away on business again? Would it be enough that I'd be dancing for myself? No, that was still only part of it. I *needed* Papa there to see what I could do.

I raced down to the kitchen, talking before I'd even got through the door.

"Maman...do you know if Papa's away on the twenty-seventh...?"

I stopped and stared.

"Ask him yourself, Jasmeen," said Maman with a smile.

I gulped. "I didn't know you were back, Papa."

"I've only just walked in!" he said, also smiling. But he looked tired as he patted my shoulder and gave me a kiss. "What's that music you're playing up there?"

"It's for the show. On the twenty-seventh. Will you be able to come?"

He flopped into a chair and closed his eyes for a moment.

"Let me make you a coffee," said Maman, flicking the switch on the kettle. "Your father's tired, Jasmeen."

"Yes, but can you just check your schedule, Papa?"

"What's the hurry, Jasmeen? Let your father have five minutes' peace."

I really wished Maman would stop interrupting. It was probably silly of me to keep going on about it, but I was so desperate to know. I spoke as quietly as possible, because it didn't seem so pushy then. "Could you just look, Papa?"

He sighed and reached into his pocket for his planner. Maman looked tense. I kept my eyes on Papa as he tapped the screen. "The twenty-seventh, you say?"

"Yes," I managed to croak.

"Looks good. What time?"

My spirits soared. "Two-thirty."

"Oh..." He frowned. My spirits sank. "Well, it depends. I'm away the previous night, but I *should* be back in time. I might miss the first part."

"Lovely," said Maman, cutting in briskly. "Can you get a cup and saucer out, Jasmeen?"

I did as I was told without saying anything else. There was no point. I couldn't change anything. It just meant that I'd be even more nervous on that day, because of wanting to do my best and also because of wondering whether Papa was in the audience or not.

4 Miss Coralie Means Business

All through school on Tuesday I was dying for the end-of-school bell to ring. It was impossible to concentrate on anything because my mind was full of the dance. I was dying to start teaching it to Poppy.

It was such a relief when we actually met in the changing room. But I couldn't help feeling disappointed to see that Tamsyn and a few others had got there early too, so they could go through their choreography.

"I think Room Two is free," I whispered to Poppy when we were bending over to put our shoes on.

"Have you two worked out your whole dance?" asked Tamsyn loudly.

"Jasmine's going to teach me now…" Poppy started to explain.

Tamsyn wrinkled her nose as though we'd made a bad smell come into the room. "You mean you haven't even tried it out together yet?"

I opened my mouth to answer, but she was already talking again. "Me and Immy and Lottie have made up a really brilliant dance. We spent nearly all Saturday doing it, didn't we, Immy?" Immy was eating potato chips and concentrating on peering over Lottie's shoulder to read her magazine, so she didn't even hear. "We're doing an ice dance. Can you imagine how it looks – all that melting and freezing? I'm so glad I thought up that idea. I just know Miss Coralie's going to love it." Then she suddenly stood up and began to slide into the sideways splits, dropping her head back dramatically. "See. Good, isn't it?"

"Yeah, fabulous!" I lowered my voice to whisper to Poppy. "Let's go into the other room. No one's in there."

Tamsyn was sliding into another ice-statue shape when we slid out.

"Okay, we start in the same positions as before and we do the running on tiptoe, only you start four beats after me," I said to Poppy, "and we finish a little further out than before..."

She nodded and we tried it, but it was hard to do with counts instead of music.

"Oh!" Tamsyn was standing in the doorway. "So that's where you went! You had the same idea as us. We thought we'd do a run-through of ours too!" She started to come into the room. Immy and Lottie were in the doorway now.

Poppy bit her lip but she didn't say anything. It was up to me.

"Well actually, the thing is, Tamsyn... Do you mind practicing yours in the hall? It's just that we've started all over again and we haven't had time to try it out together yet."

"But the hall isn't big enough," said Tamsyn.

"It doesn't matter, Tams," said Lottie from the doorway. "Let Jazz and Poppy have this room."

"We've had tons of time to practice," Immy added.

Tamsyn didn't have any choice, because the other two had gone back to the changing room, but she didn't look too happy. "It's not my fault if you two haven't bothered to practice together..." she muttered as she went out.

Poppy tried calling after her. "We have, only..."

"Never mind about Tamsyn," I said. "Let's just get on."

And we tried. I knew it was best to start at the beginning, but unfortunately that was one of the most complicated parts. After the tiptoe running, we had to stay perfectly still. This was the moment the two stars realized that they were alone in the dark sky. Then they suddenly had to burst into action as though the search for each other had begun. The sequence I'd worked out for that part was tricky for Poppy to learn, and she still hadn't got it when we heard the *révérence* music coming from Room One.

"We'll have to line up, Poppy. Our class will be starting in a minute."

"Can't we show Miss Coralie the old version, Jazz?"

"Don't worry, I'll explain..."

I sounded brave, but inside I was as nervous as a cat.

Everyone always stands up very straight when we're in the line waiting to go in. It's impossible to describe the feeling I get inside my chest when the door opens and the class before comes out. You see them go running lightly past, looking hot and tired and not saying a word to each other. And I always feel as if my heart's grown bigger.

I raised my eyebrows at Rose as she came out, which was my way of asking if she'd had a good lesson. She nodded and whispered to Poppy and me as she passed us. "My group's supposed to be doing a summer breeze, only they're complaining that I'm making it a hurricane!" Then she turned her palms up and made a face as though she didn't understand why they should say that.

"Come in, next class!" came Miss Coralie's firm voice.

Automatically I did what Miss Eleanor, my very first ballet teacher, taught me to do. I imagined I was a puppet, with the puppet master gently pulling on a thin piece of string that went in through the middle of the top of my head right inside me, down to my stomach. As the puppet master pulled, every part of me rose up out of my abdomen in the straightest line.

Miss Coralie, all in black, apart from a beautiful pale green cross-over top that matched her earrings, was standing in third position, watching us like a hawk as we ran with the lightest footsteps to the *barre*.

She waited till we were in fifth position, then said, "Good afternoon girls. Just a quick warm-up today because I'd like to see how your dances are developing. I shall be coming around from group to group. Right..." We waited for the magic words, as Mrs. Marsden, the pianist, lifted her hands ready to play the *plié* music. "*Preparation...and...*"

I love *pliés*. I don't know if it's because they're the very first thing we do at the beginning of class or because I just love them anyway.

"Nice, Jasmine," said Miss Coralie as she walked past me.

It's the very best feeling when you get a "nice" or a "good" from Miss Coralie because she's got very high standards. In fact, she used to dance with the Royal Ballet Company. And if you get a "lovely" you feel like flying with happiness.

After we'd done *battements tendus,* and some *grands battements,* Miss Coralie asked us to get into our groups and start work.

"I know it's not the same without music," she said, "but you can concentrate on technique and expression. If there's time at the end, we might see one or two groups with the music. I trust everyone has practiced since last Tuesday?" Miss Coralie's eyes passed over the groups. Poppy's elbow nudged my arm. I think she wanted me to say something. But it wasn't our turn. "Rainbow group, did you manage to get together?"

There were seven girls in one of the groups. Although Miss Coralie had said it would be best to be in small groups to make it easier to get together between lessons, she'd been so impressed with the idea of the rainbow that she'd allowed the group of seven.

The girls all nodded and one of them said they'd managed to figure out the whole dance.

"That's what I like to hear," said Miss Coralie. She gave them a small smile as though she hadn't time for a big one, then moved on to Tamsyn's group.

"We've done all of ours, too," said Tamsyn in her usual loud voice.

"Excellent," said Miss Coralie with the same half-smile. "Alexandra and Becky, how is your story of the argument between the wind and the sun going?"

"We've figured out most of it," said Alexandra, "but Becky's been out of school most of the week."

Now it was nearly our turn my mouth was getting dry. I'd thought it was going to be so easy to explain about starting all over again, but Miss Coralie didn't seem in the right mood for listening to explanations.

"Glad you're better, Becky. And the girls doing the star dance? Jasmine? Poppy?"

Poppy was nudging me. I swallowed.

"Is there a problem, you two?"

"No... We've done it all," Poppy blurted out.

"Good, let's get to work then," said Miss Coralie. Then off she went to the rainbow group.

I swallowed again and looked at Poppy. Her freckles hardly showed at all because her face was so red. I felt sorry for her, but I was determined not to go back to the old dance.

"I'll never be able to do that new part, Jazz. And then there's all the rest to learn."

"You'll be fine. Come on..."

We went over the first complicated sequence again, but Poppy was too nervous to concentrate. "It would be easier if we had the music," she said, biting her lip.

"I'll try and sing it, okay?"

But we'd hardly started when Tamsyn's voice came ringing out. "Jasmine, can you be quiet, you're ruining my concentration!" And Miss Coralie frowned at me from across the room.

But after a little while, I began to feel better.

Poppy could do the sequence really well and we'd gone on to the next part.

"Are you sure it's all right?" asked Poppy. "It doesn't feel as flowing as the way it was before."

"That's only because we haven't got the music and we haven't practiced enough together," I told her.

Then Miss Coralie was suddenly at our side.

"Okay, girls, from the top."

I really wanted to explain about how we'd made up the whole dance then completely changed it, but it was obvious from Miss Coralie's flashing eyes that she was in a big hurry, and didn't have time for talking. So we started.

Poppy was still nervous but she managed to get through the tricky section and we also did the next part. It all seemed to be over in a flash.

"What about the rest of the dance?" asked Miss Coralie.

"Well, you see, we'd already made up the

whole dance," Poppy started gabbling, "but then Jasmine decided to change it…"

Miss Coralie turned her head sharply to look at me. "Change it?"

"To make it better," I said, feeling my cheeks getting hot. "I've worked it out all the way to the end, only we didn't have time…"

Miss Coralie's eyes flickered over to the clock above the piano. "Just make sure you've finished it by next week, girls," she said in a crisp voice. Then, she clapped her hands to tell everyone in the class to come and sit down at the front.

"Now," she began briskly when everyone was quiet, "you remember that the title of the show is *Shades of Nature*, but can anyone tell me which aspect of nature has not yet been mentioned?"

We all frowned hard.

"Fish?" asked Isobel after a moment.

Miss Coralie shook her head. I heard Tamsyn snicker.

"Is it the air?" asked Immy.

"No, but that's a clever idea. I'll tell you..."

And, right at that moment, something flashed into my mind. "Is it human beings?"

"Yes, Jasmine. Human beings. People. Being born and growing up. Now, I've choreographed a dance to some music that our talented pianist, Mrs. Marsden, has written herself..." We all looked at Mrs. Marsden. She seemed a little embarrassed, as though she wasn't expecting Miss Coralie to say her name just then. "I've called it *Life*. This is going to be a dance for pupils of all ages. I'm picking one person to represent each class and the dance will form the *finale* of the show."

Every single one of us sat up a little straighter. I saw Miss Coralie and Mrs. Marsden exchange a look. It was a grown-up look. There are lots of those between Maman and Papa. And thinking that thought made my stomach fill with butterflies because I wanted to be chosen for the

Life dance so badly, but it was sure to mean extra rehearsals and I knew that my dad would never allow it.

"My choreography for the *Life* dance is full of little cameo pictures. Like this..." Miss Coralie began to move and the silence seemed to grow another layer. Very slowly, she lifted her arms and uncurled her fingers. The movement was gentler than steam rising. Then, keeping perfect balance, she rose on tiptoe and spun around twice with her skirt swirling after her. Her arms had floated high above her head but when she stopped turning they sank down into praying hands.

I went into a sort of dream imagining what the rest of the dance would look like, but then I came straight back to earth with a bang because Miss Coralie had suddenly changed back to her brisk self, and it was just as though she'd never said a word about the new dance.

"Right everybody, in your lines for the *révérence* please."

We all hurried into place on tiptoe, and were just about to start the curtsy when Miss Coralie suddenly said, "Jasmine, can you see me afterward?"

"Does that mean that you've chosen Jasmine?" Tamsyn asked. Her voice wasn't as loud as usual.

"I haven't decided yet," came the answer.

My heart banged against my ribs. Did she want to see me for a completely different reason? Was it because she was upset about our dance not being ready?

The moment the *révérence* music had finished, everyone started filing out. I could see Tamsyn out of the corner of my eye as I went to the front. She was hanging around because she wanted to hear what Miss Coralie was going to say. But Miss Coralie was talking to Mrs. Marsden and, by the time she'd finished, everyone else had gone, so Tamsyn had to go too.

A flood of nervousness came over me when I saw Miss Coralie's serious face. I stood very still except for my shaking legs.

"Jasmine," she began, "I had you in mind to represent this class in the *Life* dance..." An enormous *yessss* began to fill up my body, but seeped away faster than a balloon popping with her next words. "There are two things concerning me... First, I don't want to overload you with extra practice, because you obviously still have a fair amount to do on your *Star* dance and, second, I'll need to speak with your parents about the extra rehearsals for the *Life* dance. They'll be on Thursdays at 4:15. It's very important to attend, so if you're unable to manage these rehearsals, I'll need to know as soon as possible so that I can choose someone for your role."

The shaking in my legs pushed their way into my whole body. "Did you say that *you'll* phone my parents, Miss Coralie?"

"Yes, I will."

I nodded. I couldn't speak. My mind was racing. It was good that Miss Coralie was going to be the one to speak to Maman and Papa. If *I'd* asked, Papa would just say that Thursday was my piano-lesson day and that was that.

"Er...how many extra rehearsals will there be?"

"Three or four... And nearer the time, when we start to put the whole thing together, you'd be needed for longer because of the show being in two sections." Miss Coralie was looking at me carefully. "I'll call this evening then, Jasmine, okay?"

I nodded again. Her eyes seemed to be locked onto mine and I wondered if she could tell that I didn't think it would be any use. Papa would never let me do it, and sometimes I hated him for not letting me do what I loved most.

5 Talking in the Dark

"What is wrong, Jasmeen?"

We were going home in the car and I was hunched in the passenger seat with my arms folded. My sadness had turned to anger.

"It's not fair."

"What's not fair?"

"I've been picked to be in the most important, most special part of the whole show and there's only one person from each class and I won't be allowed to do it because of stupid old Pa..." I couldn't say the truth, because it would have made my mom angry.

"...because of stupid old piano lessons."

"Why piano?"

"Because the extra rehearsals are on Thursdays."

Maman didn't say anything. We both knew that it was really Papa stopping me, because he was the one who decided whether I had to do piano lessons or not.

I wanted to make Maman suffer for being on Papa's side, not mine. "Miss Coralie's going to call tonight, but there's no point, is there?"

"Well, we can't just expect Mrs. Waghorn to let you miss a chunk of the lessons every time there's something else going on in your life. She made it very clear when you started piano that learning any instrument is a commitment."

"But I didn't even want to learn."

Maman made a kind of snorty noise. "That's not how I remember it. You were begging to learn the piano."

"But that was before I realized how much I love ballet."

Maman set her lips in a tight thin line and stared at the road as though she was driving in a race.

I wriggled around inside my seat belt till I was facing her, knowing that I was acting like a baby. "Can't you make Papa say it's all right for me to go to one tiny little extra rehearsal every week. Pleeeeease?"

I did praying hands, but Maman had her eyes on the road, so she didn't even see.

"He let you do extra lessons last time for your exam."

I felt a ray of hope. "So you think he'd let me do it again, then?"

She laughed a tinkly laugh. "No, *chérie*. What I mean is, you can't *keep* asking him for extra this and extra that."

The ray of hope faded as I harrumphed myself back to face the front and folded my arms even tighter than before. Now I was really acting like a baby. But I couldn't help it. "It's not fair."

When we got home, I tried again. Mom was making dinner and humming at the same time, except that I kept interrupting the humming.

"What time's he coming home, anyway?"

"Do you mean your father?"

"Yes!"

I couldn't help snapping because it was obvious I meant Papa, but I straight away wished I hadn't because Maman gave me a quick look with her eyebrows raised and the rest of her face set hard. I hate it when she does that. It's like a telling off without any words, which is worse than an ordinary telling off. She must have really had enough of me.

"What time's Papa coming home?" I tried again in a quiet voice.

"He may be late. And he will be tired."

I was used to Papa being tired. As well as

being a doctor, he also does operations. That's when he gets the most tired and comes home with his eyelids drooping almost shut.

"What if you tell him that this is the very last time I'll ever *ever* ask for extra rehearsals?"

"That's what I said last term. How many sausages?"

My anger came back. "I don't know…it doesn't matter, does it?"

Out of the corner of my eye, I could see Maman getting her face ready to wear that mask look. She was standing perfectly still with the spatula in her hand. I thought I'd better give her a proper answer. "Two, please."

When the phone rang later, I sat with my thumbs pressed against each other, and a little prayer going on inside my head as Maman answered it.

"Hello, Miss Coralie… Yes, Jasmine's told me." I wished I could hear what Miss Coralie was saying on the other end. Maman's face wasn't giving me any clues. She just kept nodding and saying, "I see." Eventually, she said, "Well, I'll have to talk to her father, but the trouble is that Jasmine has piano lessons on Thursday."

I held my breath and waited to see what she'd say next. It seemed like a very long wait. "Yes, yes, of course. I'll let you know tomorrow... All right... Thank you very much. Goodbye."

I gave Maman a fierce look but didn't speak. There was nothing to say.

"It's not the end of the world, Jasmeen. You're still going to be dancing with Poppy and that's very special, isn't it?"

Not as special as doing the Life *dance,* I thought, but what I said was, "Can you ask Papa tonight?"

"Yes, of course. Then I'll phone Miss Coralie tomorrow."

It was really difficult making my eyes stay open as I lay in bed listening for the sound of Papa's key in the lock. I knew he was going to be late, but I never thought he'd be *this* late. I'd left my night-light on and I could see that the time on my Nutcracker clock was twenty-five past ten. Maybe I'd better give in and go to sleep. It was just that Maman had promised to ask him about the rehearsals when he got in. My plan was to sneak out onto the stairs to listen.

I must have been practically asleep, because I suddenly jumped at the sound of the front door closing. In a flash, I was sitting upright with staring eyes, listening with all my might. It was silly. I knew that really. She wouldn't say anything the moment he walked through the door, would she? But...

Creak! That was the next-to-top stair. Oh, no! What if it was Papa? What if he popped his head around my door? I knew they both often did that. As fast as I'd shot up, I crashed back down again, snapping my eyes shut, pretending to be asleep. But lying all stiff and straight like a dead person, it was impossible. I could feel my eyes twitching because they were screwed up too tightly.

"Jasmine, I can see perfectly well that you're awake." His voice was low.

My heart was really beating as I opened my eyes and sat up slowly, saying the first words that came into my head. "I couldn't get to sleep, Papa..."

He looked a little sorry for me, and that made me keep on. "You see, I was worrying...about Miss Coralie..."

The very second the words were out of my mouth, I wished I could take them back.. But I couldn't stop now. "The trouble is, she really really wants me to have a special part in her show..."

"I know, Jasmine. We've been through this once. I'm going to do my best to make it, remember? It's the twenty-seventh, isn't it?" His voice sounded gentle and kind. And now he was smiling in a tired sort of way. But he obviously didn't realize that we were talking about different things. He was in such a good mood that I just couldn't help trying.

"Miss Coralie's chosen me out of the whole class to dance in the *finale* dance. There's only one of us from each class and she's done the choreography herself. There are just a few extra rehearsals on...Thursdays." I ran my words together so that the *Thursday* word didn't stand out too much. "I told Miss Coralie that I was sure you wouldn't mind as it is so important..."

"A few?"

He didn't sound so soft and tired now.

"Three or four... And the full rehearsals might be a little longer." I held my breath.

Papa sighed. "It's far too late to be having this kind of conversation now, Jasmine. You need to get to sleep or you'll be in no fit state to concentrate at school tomorrow." As he closed the door behind him, it felt as though a light had gone out inside my head. He hadn't exactly said no, but I can always tell when he's on his way to a no. Tears were tickling the sides of my face. I never knew they could squeeze themselves out of closed eyes.

6 Extraterrestrial Nutcrackers

"Hey, that's so cool!" It was Saturday afternoon. Rose was lying on her stomach on my bed. Poppy and I had just showed her the finished dance with the music. "You're really talented," she added, jumping up. Then she suddenly put on a totally snobby, over-the-top voice. "But not as talented as me!" It was obvious that she was pretending to be Tamsyn. "Now *I'm* the only one in the class to be doing the *Life* dance. Ha, ha. That means the audience will be looking at *me* more than ever!"

We both giggled. "You sound just like her," I said.

Rose sat on the floor. "Don't you mind not being in the *Life* dance, Jazz?"

I sighed. "Not any more... You see, I knew I'd never be allowed."

That wasn't totally true. Sometimes, on my own, I feel completely miserable about it. At other times I feel really mad, especially when I think of how Papa went off early the next morning after he'd talked to me that night. So it had been Maman who'd told me that I wasn't allowed. Maman phoned Miss Coralie and, the next lesson, we heard that Tamsyn had been chosen. But mostly I'm over it now. And I'm excited about our *Starshine* dance. I get such a wonderful feeling every time we rehearse it.

Rose was narrowing her eyes and clenching her fists. "Well, if I were you, I'd be so mad I'd have to throw things around the room and scream the place down. When I see your dad I'm going to tell him off – big time."

"You'd better not, or you'll never be allowed in this house again," said Poppy, looking worried.

Rose didn't reply. She'd spotted one of my books on the book shelf and was pulling it out. At first I thought she was going to hurl it out of my bedroom window but instead she started flipping through the pages. A moment later she was really glued to it. "Hey, this is saying all the reasons why ballet's supposed to be so good for you," she said, looking up. "You ought to show your dad this, you know, Jazz?"

I sighed. "There's no point. You can't argue with him. He always thinks he knows best."

"But what about all these things it says here?" Rose stabbed the book with her finger. "Stamina, strength, limberness, coordination, balance, posture, concentration, aural skills, memory, confidence, creative skills and general awareness. I'm sure your dad would change his mind if he knew all that, Jazz."

"He wouldn't. Honestly. He thinks exams are more important than that whole list."

"Well, anyway…" Rose suddenly started squirming around. "I'm going to the bathroom."

The moment she'd gone out, Poppy turned to me. "Where *is* your dad?"

"It's okay, he's at the gym."

"Whew! I'm just so scared that Rose'll say something and…"

But Poppy never finished the sentence because we both clearly heard Papa's voice downstairs.

I froze. "Oh no! He's back already!" Then I shot out of my room to try and grab Rose before she could say anything.

Uh-oh! Too late. As I leaned over the stair railing, I saw Rose standing in the hall with Papa. Poppy was at my side in a flash. She clapped her hand to her mouth and we both hung there, watching and listening, with our hearts hammering.

"Hello, Doctor Ayed."

I nearly gasped out loud. Rose was smiling and sticking out her hand.

Papa looked very puzzled as he shook her hand. "And you are...?"

"Rose Bedford. Jazz's friend." Then she pointed to the photo hanging up behind Papa. "Wow! You were really handsome when you were young, weren't you?"

"Well, I..." said Papa. I'd never heard him sound as though he didn't know what to say next.

"And you don't look at all like a scary person either."

This time I really did gasp.

"I...er..."

Rose didn't wait for an answer, just kept on talking. "It doesn't matter. I was just wondering why you didn't let Jazz do the extra rehearsals for the *Life* dance. She's really sad, you know."

Poppy drew up close to me. I could feel her arm trembling and I knew mine was doing the same.

Papa's eyes lost their puzzled look and he spoke quickly, as though he wasn't interested in the conversation any more. "Jasmine learns piano... She can't do everything." Then he started to walk away.

"But ballet's the most important thing in her whole life, Doctor Ayed."

Poppy clutched my trembling arm. Papa stopped walking and turned around. He looked at Rose with a sort of half-smile and spoke in a patient voice, as though she was a little stupid. "Look, I really don't think it's any of your business, Rose."

"She doesn't look at all scared," Poppy whispered right into my ear.

I didn't reply. I was too busy listening to Rose. And I couldn't believe my ears. "Well, actually it *is*, Doctor Ayed, because Jazz is my friend."

Poppy and I both gasped. Rose had really done it now.

Papa jerked his head sharply. I saw his eyes flash. Rose didn't seem to notice. She just kept talking away.

"And another thing... You see, I was reading this book all about ballet. And it said that ballet can really help you with things like schoolwork and *especially* exams."

I gulped and felt Poppy's shoulders tensing. We looked at each other in alarm. Poppy's face was very pale and her freckles really stood out.

Rose was holding up the thumb of her left hand ready to start counting off the list. "This is what ballet's good for, in case you didn't know...coordination, memory, concentration, posture..." She was reeling off all the words from the book. It was incredible that she'd remembered them so well. "...aural awareness, stamina, strength, limberness, balance...er... confidence, creative skills, general awareness..."

Papa was staring at the carpet. I think he was waiting till Rose had definitely finished before he went crazy.

I held my breath. Rose was silent. No wonder. She'd come to the end of the list.

But then, a second later, she was ticking her fingers off again as she came out with more words. Only she was just saying the first things that came into her head. "*Assemblé, pirouette, arabesque*, poltergeist, *chassé plié, perspiration...*"

I looked at Papa. His head had dropped right onto his chest. Rose was going to get it! And whatever was she saying now?

"...energy, *révérence, pas de chat*, expression, *battement tendu*, adjective and extraterrestrial nutcrackers."

"What?" I squeaked, clutching Poppy and waiting for the big thunderclap to come.

Then I got the shock of my life because Papa's head came up and I could see tears swimming in his eyes. He seemed to be shaking. What was happening? Surely Rose hadn't managed to make him cry, had she? I grabbed Poppy's hand and pulled her downstairs. But, as we reached the bottom stair, Papa collapsed against the wall and let out a noise that reminded me of a happy chimpanzee I'd once seen on television. And that was when I realized that *my dad* was laughing. He was actually laughing his head off.

Rose broke into a huge grin. "So you never did change into a scary person, after all. You're just pretending, aren't you?"

Papa shook his head at Rose. "You...are ...incredible!" he spluttered through his big chuckles.

Then Maman appeared from the kitchen looking completely puzzled, with a tea towel in her hands. "What's so funny?"

Papa turned to her and pointed at Rose. "This girl ought to be on the stage!"

Rose looked puzzled. "I'm not really much good at ballet..."

"Ballet? No, no, no. Being funny. Stand-up comic!" He looked at Maman again. "She's something else, this girl! You should have heard her!"

Rose eyed Papa suspiciously. "So...you're not sorry about not letting Jazz do the extra rehearsals?"

Papa didn't seem to hear her. He just did one more little chuckle. "Extraterrestrial nutcrackers indeed!"

Maman started giggling.

I looked at Rose. All the braveness seemed to have gone out of her. I suddenly felt really angry with Papa for laughing like that when all Rose had been trying to do was to help me. And he was just ignoring what she'd said completely. I went over to her and put my arm around her. "Come on, Rose. Let's go back up." As we turned, I made sure that I spoke in no more than a whisper. "Thank you for trying."

When we were halfway upstairs, she suddenly pulled away from me and her chin went up. "Never mind, Jazz, your dad might be able to stop you doing extra rehearsals, but he can never stop you loving ballet, can he?"

I turned around to see if Papa had heard. He had his hand on the kitchen door and Maman was saying something to him, so I didn't think he could have. But when we got to the top I looked down and got a surprise. Papa's hand was still on the kitchen door and he was staring at the wall in a kind of trance. Then he turned to Maman and said, "Out of the mouths of babes."

I'd no idea what he meant, but it didn't matter anyway. Papa still thought he knew best, so there was no point in talking about it. There wasn't even any point in him coming to the show really. Nothing would change his mind. Nothing.

7 The Big Day

As the day of the show drew nearer and nearer, Poppy, Rose and I grew more and more excited and nervous. And there was another reason to be excited now, as well. Miss Coralie had told us that she'd arranged for a lady called Miss Bird to come and judge the show. Apparently, Miss Bird used to be a real professional dancer when she was young. At the end of the show she was going to give out three special awards.

Tamsyn's hand had shot up straight away. "Will they be individual awards, Miss Coralie?"

"I've left that up to Miss Bird, but I should

imagine so, yes. She'll be considering performance quality, technique and, in the case of the Tuesday students, choreography too."

I suddenly thought back to the lesson when Miss Coralie had watched Poppy and me do our dance together all the way through with the music for the first time. We hadn't danced our best because we'd both been feeling nervous, but I'd been able to tell from the look in Miss Coralie's eyes that she'd really liked it. She'd stayed completely silent at the end for a long, long moment, and then spoken with her breath more than her voice. "That was really beautiful."

I'd felt a big lump in my throat when she'd said that and ever since I hadn't cared half so much about not being in the *Life* dance. I'd just practiced and practiced *Starshine* until I thought I couldn't dance it any better. Tamsyn had told us in the changing room that in one of the rehearsals for the *Life* dance, Miss Coralie had made her show all the other girls how to do one particular part. That was the only time I felt jealous because that might have been me. But then I quickly shook the stupid jealous thoughts away. Tamsyn might have been a show-off, but she was also a brilliant dancer. Everyone was sure that she was going to get one of Miss Bird's merit awards.

Papa had never said anything to me about Rose, but I'd asked Maman the meaning of "Out of the mouths of babes" because I couldn't get those words out of my head. She'd said it was an expression which meant that sometimes children – even very young children – happen to hit on a simple truth, where adults haven't been able to. Once or twice, I'd wondered what that simple truth might be, but most of the time I was too excited and nervous about the show and whether Papa would be there to think about anything else.

Eventually the day came.

"This is really really it! I can't believe it!" said Poppy, clutching my hands.

We were waiting in line to have our make-up put on. Our costumes were absolutely beautiful. Both of us were wearing deep-blue, sleeveless leotards with a glittery silver edge to the neck and matching elastic belts. From the belts floated strips of silky, silvery-blue ribbons. Our ballet shoes were black. Our hair was scraped back and we both wore tiny sparkling crowns.

"Smile for the camera!" said Lottie, who was going around taking everyone's picture.

Poppy and I put our arms around each other and our heads together for the photo. When she'd taken it, Lottie said, "You two look beautiful, you know, especially because of Jasmine being so dark and Poppy being so pale."

Poppy and I didn't know what to say, so we just kept smiling and when Lottie had gone we did a thumb-thumb. I'd lost count of the number of times we'd done that in the last hour while we'd been in here getting ready and warming up. It was partly for good luck in our dance, but also partly because we were hoping that my dad would be there. Maman had come on her own and said that Papa would be joining her just as soon as he got back from his conference.

The changing room was really the small hall in the Community Center, but it was just the right size for all the Tuesday girls, all the little ones and a few older ones. The students who were fourteen or older were upstairs in a sort of staff lounge because there weren't many of them.

The younger ones were already changed, with their make-up on, because they were the first to go on stage. They'd been gathered together by Miss Eleanor and Miss Melissa, who are the other two teachers at Miss Coralie's, and taken to wait in the wings. I guessed that some of them were probably already in their positions on the stage behind the big, heavy velvet curtain. Just thinking that thought made a swarm of butterflies come fluttering into my stomach.

Rose was on the other side of the room practicing her dance with the other two girls in her group. As soon as Poppy and I had our make-up on, we went through the first part of our own dance.

"Your knee's not stretched on that *rond de jambe*, Poppy," said Tamsyn, going past us at that moment.

Poppy went red. I wanted to tell Tamsyn to mind her own business, but I didn't dare. Anyway, Miss Coralie had come into the room.

"Right, everybody." She clapped her hands. "All eyes on me, please." She didn't really have to say it. We were already silent, waiting to hear what was happening. "The show begins in less than five minutes. From now on, we talk only in whispers, because loud talking in here will be heard from the audience. I've had a peep through the curtain and the auditorium is packed." Everyone nodded nervously. "Three minutes before you're needed, you'll be called by myself, Miss Melissa or Miss Eleanor. Immediately before you perform, take two or three slow deep breaths and focus hard on what you're about to do, then try to imagine you're growing wings and are about to fly across the world."

My heart grew inside my chest when Miss Coralie said those words. I knew exactly what she meant. I couldn't wait to be on the stage now. Absolutely couldn't wait.

8 Growing Wings and Flying

"On you go, Rose," said Miss Coralie. "Deep breath."

For once, Rose's footsteps didn't make a sound as she tiptoed to center front stage. Poppy was in the opposite back wing from me. We gave each other shaky smiles as the heavy curtains slid slowly apart and Rose's voice rang out over the whole hall.

The sky is deep and dark.
The sky is dark and deep.
The world is still and silent.
Everyone's asleep.

Jasmine's Lucky Star

Who is strong enough to drag
the heavy black away?
Or peel it, chip it, little by little
until it turns to day?

Glinting in the blackness is
a single twinkling star,
Trying to drizzle silver dust –
not getting very far.

"I need a friend to help me.
If we touch we'll make a flare of light!"
And so the star set off to search.
And search and search that lonely night.

This was it! The poem had finished. Rose was standing perfectly still, the audience were clapping and my heart was thumping. Somewhere out there in the darkness was Maman. And maybe Papa too. Maybe. I wouldn't know, because I couldn't look for him when I was dancing. Anyway, it would be too dark to see.

I took two slow deep breaths as I watched Rose walk off to the front wing. Then, as the music started, something magic made me rise onto my toes. It must have been magic because I don't remember telling myself to do it. I ran on tiptoe right across to the opposite front corner of the stage and sank to my knees, knowing without looking that Poppy would be doing the same thing, four beats later, from her side of the stage. And, from that moment on, I really felt as though I *was* a lonely star in the sky.

I wasn't nervous at all any more, just floaty and strong but light as a feather as I danced and danced, better than I'd ever danced before. And though I knew Poppy was there, she didn't seem like Poppy, she seemed like just another lonely star swirling and swooping in the deep, black night.

As the end of the music came with a string of

glittering notes that floated into the air, we held our final positions in front center stage. I was facing stage right and Poppy stage left. This was the most difficult part of all. My heart was really thumping from dancing with all my energy, but trying to make it look smooth and easy and liquid. And now we had to balance on our front foot and raise the back one in a low *arabesque*. There was so much to think about – turning out, not bending the supporting knee, pulling up out of your ribs, not rolling on your feet, keeping your alignment, not leaning forward too much, pointing your toes, not lifting your shoulders, tilting your head to look out to the audience...

And then I couldn't resist it. I just had to look. My eyes flitted over the rows of people all smiling and clapping and clapping. I saw Maman straight away, but there was an empty seat beside her. My body felt suddenly drained. Papa hadn't made it. I let my *arabesque* drop and Poppy did the same because we'd agreed to hold it as long as we could and when the first one dropped it, the other one would do the same. Usually it was Poppy who dropped first. But this time it was me. I just didn't have the heart to hold it for another second.

As we straightened up to do our curtsy, my eyes flitted to the back of the auditorium and there, standing up tall, with a proud smile on his face, was Papa. He met my eyes and gave me a double thumbs-up, then started everyone off in another burst of applause. All my energy came flooding back and I wished I could do the whole dance again, and this time I'd hold the *arabesque* forever. Papa had seen me and he was proud of me.

I sank into the curtsy at exactly the same moment as Poppy and then the curtains swished closed in front of us.

9 The Awards

We were all sitting on the stage facing the audience. The show had finished and Miss Bird had come up onto the stage too. She'd been sitting in the third row right in the middle. Papa was in the seat beside Maman now. I'd given them both a little wave and then started concentrating on Miss Bird.

"I knew she was the judge," Tamsyn whispered into the back of my neck. "I spotted her right away, you know."

I didn't turn around because Miss Bird was about to start talking. She was half facing us and half facing the audience, so she could talk to everyone at once.

"Ssh!" said Rose.

But Tamsyn didn't *ssh*. "Can I squeeze in next to you?" she said. "I can't see anything from back here."

We hadn't been squashed when we were standing, but everyone took up more room when they were sitting down. Tamsyn pushed in between me and Lottie. She was kneeling, her back up very straight, blocking the view of the girls behind her.

Miss Bird welcomed the audience and said it was a privilege to be there. She talked about the new auditorium and the lovely stage and how we'd all made it seem like a real theater because of our wonderful dancing. Then she said she was going to announce who had won the three special merit awards.

"I had a very difficult time trying to select just three people, and I found it virtually impossible to pick out individuals from the smaller groups, particularly in the case of groups working closely together. My first award is a most appropriate one, because the three little girls concerned performed a dance that must have been especially for me..." She broke into a big smile. "*The Dance of the Birds!* So well done to Milly Landon, Phoebe Wright and Rachel Warder!"

We all burst into applause as Milly, Rachel and Phoebe got up and went over to Miss Bird. Miss Coralie must have told the little ones to curtsy if they won an award, because all three girls did cute curtsys. I heard some people in the audience say "Aaah!"

"But that's just one award, isn't it?" hissed Tamsyn right in my ear. "There are still two more to come, aren't there?"

I didn't even look at her, just nodded. She'd already stopped clapping and was kneeling even straighter.

"My second award is for an individual," said

Miss Bird. "This is a girl who I'm sure will go far. I want you to remember her name because I think one day we'll see it in lights." Miss Bird left a big, long pause before she said the name.

"Bet it's Katie," Poppy whispered to me.

"Or Tamsyn," I whispered back.

"Katie Denver, please come and receive your award."

A big cheer went up as Katie stood up slowly. She's fourteen but she's very shy and you could see she was embarrassed because she looked down at the stage as she walked to Miss Bird. I was clapping so much my hands were hurting, but Tamsyn was hardly clapping at all. I think she wanted to get to the last award.

Katie shook hands and did a tiny little bob curtsy. She looked so graceful. I agreed with Miss Bird. One day Katie would be a real ballerina. When I saw her dancing, I thought there was probably no hope in the world for my ballerina dream to come true.

"And my last award is also for a group," Miss Bird was saying.

"A group? She's not going to give the award to *everyone* in the *Life* dance, surely!" said Tamsyn, in a loud whisper.

"Ssh!" hissed Rose.

"A very talented group indeed." She looked around all of us and her eyes seemed to have settled on Tamsyn. But then she must have been saying the wrong words. "And a very small group! Well done to Poppy Vernon and Jasmine Ayed."

I gasped.

"Huh!" said Tamsyn, only it came out like a snort.

I couldn't move! I just sat there in a trance. It couldn't be us. What about Tamsyn?

But Poppy was already on her feet. "Come on," she whispered. Her cheeks were bright pink. "It's us!"

"Go on, Jazz!" said Rose, patting me on the back really hard. "You brilliant dancers!"

Poppy and I walked over to Miss Bird and shook hands like Katie had done, then did the same bob curtsy as the audience started clapping.

Miss Bird looked tiny close-up. She was only a little taller than me even with high heels on. Her cheek bones were high and sharp. I couldn't stop staring at them. Her face was like a heart with two dark eyes in the middle. Her eyelashes were thick and curly.

"Congratulations, stars," she whispered to us. "And did you make up the poem too?"

"Poppy did," I said.

"Quite beautiful. I'd like to have a copy of it, if that's all right."

We nodded even harder. And smiled and smiled. This really *was* like a ballerina dream come true.

10 Me and My Dad

When Poppy, Rose and I had gotten changed, we went across the stage and down the front steps to find our parents. It felt strange going through the curtain and seeing no audience. All the chairs had been moved to the sides and everyone was standing around talking.

I spotted Maman right away, talking with Poppy and Rose's mothers, but I couldn't see Papa. Then Poppy nudged me and, when I followed her gaze, I saw that he was standing on his own at the side looking at the program.

"See you in a minute, Poppy."

I felt shy going over to him for some reason, but the shyness disappeared when he gave me a huge smile.

"Did you see me do the whole dance?"

"Well, I'm not sure..." I felt a jab of disappointment. "I think it might have been someone else I was watching actually... Someone from the Royal Ballet School!" He gave me a wink and pointed to his program. "Though it does say Jasmine Ayed here, so I guess it must have been you."

Happiness sizzled through my whole body. Papa had *really* thought I was good.

"Clever girl," he said, kissing the top of my head. "I'm very proud of you."

And that's when Maman came over with Poppy and Rose and their mothers. A moment later, Miss Bird joined us too.

Her face crinkled into a smile and she started telling us about four tickets that she'd been sent by her daughter to go and see her dancing in a ballet called *Rhonda*.

"I was going to ask my other daughter to come along with her husband and their little girl," said Miss Bird. "But, of course, they've seen Anna dancing many many times, so it's not such a treat for them..."

I couldn't help interrupting, I just had to know... "It's not Anna Lane, is it?"

Miss Bird broke into a big beaming smile. "Yes, it is. So you've heard of my daughter!"

Poppy and I turned very slowly toward each other and, if my eyes looked as big as hers at that moment, they must have looked absolutely enormous.

"So, I was wondering if you three might like to come and see the ballet with me. I'm sure Anna would be delighted to give you a guided tour backstage afterward. It's on the nineteenth of next month."

Everyone started thanking Miss Bird like crazy. But Papa was looking at Maman with a frown on his face. "Isn't that the weekend your mother invited us all to visit?"

I knew there'd be something. There always was. I hung my head, feeling a terrible sadness growing in me.

"So does that mean I can't go?" I asked in a small voice.

"I'm afraid..." Papa began, then he suddenly broke off and looked at Rose. She was staring at him hard. He narrowed his eyes, as though he was remembering something, then looked back at me.

"I think we can explain to Mami that something rather special has come up and see if we can't rearrange things."

Rose and Poppy and I all looked at each other, eyes wide.

"You mean...I can go?" I dared to ask.

Papa nodded. He was giving me a special smile.

"You must be very proud of Jasmine," said

Miss Bird. "Such a talented girl, both at dancing and choreography." She patted Papa's hand as though he was a little boy. "She's going to go far, I know."

The three moms had gone off into their own conversation by now. Poppy, Rose and I were looking at the silver medal that Poppy and I had won. Papa was looking at the floor and, even though his voice was scarcely more than a whisper, I could hear a little of what he was saying to Miss Bird.

"I had it pointed out to me recently that if someone loves something more than anything in the world, there's absolutely nothing anyone can do to stop that love. I was very struck by those words." Rose and I looked at each other, open-mouthed. "And then this afternoon, standing at the back of the audience, I realized something else. If someone loves something as much as that, why would anyone *want* to try and stop them loving it?"

"Wise words, Mr. Ayed," said Miss Bird, patting Papa's arm again.

"Er...*Doctor* Ayed, actually," said Rose, stepping forward.

"Oh, I'm sorry..." began Miss Bird.

"Not at all," said Papa.

Then his arm reached out for me, so I snuggled into him and he squeezed my shoulder.

I felt like dancing around the whole place singing at the top of my voice, but I didn't want to move from where I was. So I just smiled at my two friends and they both came closer to me. That meant we could do our thumb-thumb. Only this time it wasn't for luck, it was for *yesssssssssssssssss!*

The End ✳

✳   ✳

✳   ✳

Rose's
Big
Decision

My grateful thanks to Sue Downey
for all her help.

1 Pulled in Two Directions

Hi! I'm Rose and I'm in a big hurry because I keep putting my leotard on the wrong way. First it was inside out and then back to front. This changing room should have a few more mirrors in it so people can see what they look like when they're getting changed. Then they wouldn't make mistakes. In fact, I think I might suggest that to Miss Coralie.

Actually, I know I *won't* suggest it to Miss Coralie, because no one in this ballet school would ever dream of suggesting *anything* to Miss Coralie. You don't talk to anyone during class and you *definitely* don't talk to Miss Coralie. When I remember when I first started ballet I feel very embarrassed, because I didn't realize about not talking and I just said anything I felt like saying. I didn't even want to *be* at ballet back then. I absolutely hated it. But then I met Poppy and Jasmine and gradually, little by little, I found that I liked it after all.

I'm not very good at it, but Poppy and Jasmine are giving me extra lessons to try to make me better. Then I'll be in the same class as them. Well, that's what *they* think. Personally, I think there's about as much chance of that happening as there is of the moon turning purple.

"You'd better hurry!" said one of the girls in my class, pushing open the changing-room door. "Miss Coralie's going to call us in any minute now."

I pulled my hair through a hairband and twisted it into a bun. "Can you save me a place in the line?"

She nodded and went out while I rammed a few hairpins through the bun, then rummaged round in my bag for my shoes. I don't even know that girl's name because, when you only meet up once a week and you're not supposed to talk in class, you don't get to know people very well.

The reason I got to know Poppy is because we're in the same year at school. She was already friends with Jasmine but they kind of let me in, and now we're all best friends together. I call us a triplegang.

I pushed my hairband on and rushed out of the changing room, taking a quick glance at myself in the mirror by the door. What a mess! I hate my leotard. It's way too big for me and I look really silly in it. How come all my clothes are too big for me? Well, I know the answer to that. It's because I always have to wear my big brothers' old jeans and T-shirts when they grow out of them. I don't mind that too much, but I feel stupid wearing a leotard that's too big.

I suppose it's really my fault. I shouldn't have refused to go with Mom to buy it. It's just that I was feeling so mad about having to do ballet in the first place that I told Mom there was no need for me to try on the leotard. She could just get one that looked as though it would fit.

"Come in, class," came Miss Coralie's strict voice as I squashed into the line in front of the girl who'd saved me a place.

We all started to move forward in silence. When you get to the door you're supposed to run in on tiptoe to a place at the *barre*. I was all ready to do my best running when I happened to look down and notice that I hadn't tucked the little drawstrings into one of my shoes, so I quickly bent down to do it. Of course that made the girl behind fall into me, so I toppled forward and didn't make a very good entrance.

Luckily, Miss Coralie was watching the girls at the end of the *barre* so she didn't notice me, but I think Mrs. Marsden, the pianist, did. I saw her frowning in my direction. I put my hand on the *barre*, then quickly took it off again because you're not supposed to do that until the preparation, so I concentrated on getting my hands exactly right, with my little fingers near my legs. Then I stood up straight in fifth position and said to myself what I always say to myself at the beginning of class. *Please let today be the day that Miss Coralie says* lovely *to me.* Twice I've had a *Good, Rose,* and three times I've had a *nice,* but they were all ages ago, and I've never had a *lovely. Lovely* is the very best word that Miss Coralie can say. It means she's really *really* impressed. I'd be in heaven if I got a *lovely,* but these days I just seem to get corrected.

"*Preparation* and..." said Miss Coralie. The music started and we all prepared to second then began the *plié* exercise as Miss Coralie watched us with her eagle eyes. She was walking slowly around the room, saying the counts to the beat of the music, and other things too, in the same rhythm: "And *one* and *two* and *lift* up *Becky* and *turn* out *Rose* and *seven* and *eight...*"

Great! I thought I *was* turning out. The trouble is that I'm doing so much extra gym at the moment that my feet aren't in the habit of turning out, because you work in straight lines for gym. I'll just have to concentrate harder than ever so I don't get mixed up and think I'm doing gym when I'm supposed to be doing ballet.

"...and *nice* work *Ellie*, and *close* in *fifth...*"

I was good at fifth position and I really focused on turning out and not arching my back, which is something else that Miss Coralie has started mentioning quite a lot recently. Surely I'll get a *lovely* now, I thought to myself, or at least a *good.*

But Miss Coralie was completely silent, joining in at the front. I wished I could turn my head to really watch her instead of just out of the corner of my eye, because she looks like a true ballerina when she does dance steps. It's no wonder. I mean, she was once a soloist with the Royal Ballet. I knew I couldn't turn and watch her though, because even your head has to be in a certain position for every single ballet exercise. There's so much to think about all the time.

"Soften your elbow, Rose. You're not doing gym now."

Oh, no! Not again! It seems like the moment I stop thinking about any part of my body, even for a microsecond, it goes straight into gym mode by mistake. It's really beginning to get on my nerves. Still, it'll be better once the gym competition's over and I go back to gym class once a week. Only two and a half weeks to go. A little shiver tickled the hairs on my arms when I had that thought, because I'm really nervous about the gym competition. But excited, too.

When we do center work I have to concentrate even harder than for the *barre*. I've just about learned all the French names for the steps and the different positions and directions and everything, but, as Miss Coralie often says, it's no good just coming to class once a week, you have to practice at home in-between as well.

I'm lucky because Poppy helps me at school during break times and after lunch, and we often get together with Jasmine on the weekend too. All we ever do when we're together is practice ballet and talk about it, or dress up and make up dances and tell each other our ballerina dreams. Well, the other two tell each other their ballerina dreams. Personally, I haven't got any. That's because I'd never be good enough to be a ballerina in a million years, so I just listen to *their* dreams. And anyway, everyone thinks I'm going to be a gymnast when I grow up, which would be great. All the same, my mom and dad can't believe how much ballet has "grown on me" as Mom puts it, in such a short time.

It all started when I opened my birthday card

from Gran and saw the little message inside, which said that her present to me was ballet lessons.

I remember my jaw hanging so far down I wasn't sure that I'd ever be able to shut my mouth again. I really think I must have been the most disappointed person in the whole world at that moment. But Mom was raising her eyebrows for me to say thank you to Gran, and Gran was smiling so I had to swallow my disappointment and try to look happy.

"Thanks, Gran."

"You don't have to pretend, dear. I know you're not impressed!" She'd chuckled like crazy.

I'd really wanted to say: *No, I am NOT impressed. Why did you get me something that you knew I'd hate?* But I just said, "Well, I'm not sure if I'll like it all that much."

"No, dear, course you aren't sure. That's because you've never tried it. But I've got a good feeling about it!"

"Gran used to do ballet, you know," Mom said, as though that would make it better. *Ha ha.*

The thought of having to go to ballet lessons was bad enough, because everyone knows I'm the tomboy sort of girl and not the ballet sort, so, for a start, my brothers would tease me more than ever. But, to make matters worse, Gran had specially booked me in at the strictest ballet school for miles around – the Coralie Charlton School of Ballet.

She'd given me another present, too. It was one of those little Russian dolls, made of brightly painted wood, that you pull apart in the middle and you find another doll inside, and then another inside that one, and a really teensy one on the very inside.

"It's lovely, isn't it?" said Mom with worried eyes. (She knew how I felt about dolls, you see.) But, actually, she didn't have to worry because I thought it was wicked, and I couldn't stop taking all the little dolls out and putting them back in again.

"The doll reminds me of you," Gran had said, twinkling, "because she's got a lot more inside her than she thinks she has!" Then she'd started chuckling again.

I hadn't got the faintest idea what Gran was talking about, but I gave her a big grin anyway, and thanked her again.

When I'd done a few weeks at ballet and I didn't hate it any more, Gran started asking me to show her all the steps. At first, I didn't want to because I wasn't much good at it, and I thought Gran might get bored watching and think she'd wasted her money on me. But she went into a smiley daydream when I was doing the exercises and said, "I could watch you all day, dear." And that made me feel as though I was better than I really was.

I love it when Gran comes to visit now, because she's the only person in my family who's interested in ballet. Mom's always too busy and Dad thinks it's a waste of space, and my brothers just tease me about it and call me a *twirly girly* and things like that. But Gran can even remember the names of the steps from when she was a girl. We usually go up to my room, and while I'm getting changed into my leotard, she looks at all my gym trophies and sometimes gives them a polish. Gran knows where I won every single one of them because she always comes with Mom and Dad to watch when I do competitions. I'm so lucky having the grandmother I've got.

"You're arching your back, Rose."

Miss Coralie's voice made me jump. She was frowning at me, so I quickly corrected myself and she gave me one of her *that'll-do* nods. I sighed without letting it show. We were more than halfway through the lesson and I hadn't even gotten a *nice* let alone a *lovely*. That was gym's fault. But what am I supposed to do?

I love gym and I want to do well in the competition. That's why I've got to practice so hard.

I sighed again. Pleasing Miss Coralie *and* my gym teacher was impossible.

2 Not Enough Oomph

It was Wednesday morning recess. Poppy was waiting for me by the door. Her face broke into a big smile when I came into the playground.

"Hi! I thought you might have gotten kept in again."

I grinned at her. "Don't worry, I was just finishing my apple."

"So, tell me what happened in your lesson."

After my ballet class, Miss Coralie teaches grade five, so I always see Jasmine and Poppy lining up in the hall when I'm going back into the changing room. There's no time to talk, and anyway their line is supposed to be silent, but they always do questioning eyebrows to find out if I got a *lovely* or not. (They know I'm desperate for Miss Coralie to say that magic word to me.) Yesterday after class, I shook my head to show them that I hadn't got one, same as usual, and they both looked disappointed, same as usual, but then I wrinkled my nose as well, which was my way of telling them that it had been worse than that.

"It was just that Miss Coralie corrected me more than usual."

Poppy put her arm around me and didn't say anything for a moment. I knew why. It was because she was trying to think of something kind to say. "Never mind. It's only because she thinks you're good and she wants you to get better."

"I think she's fed up with always having to say the same things to me."

Poppy looked a little anxious then. "Is it

because you keep standing like a gymnast?"

I nodded. "It must be because I'm doing so much extra gym right now and it's getting me into the habit of arching my back and straightening my arms too much and all that kind of stuff. It never used to matter before I started ballet."

"Do you think Miss Coralie minds?"

I shrugged. "I don't know. I just have to keep saying, 'Come on brain, remember it's ballet today.' And then when I'm at gym practice, 'Forget about ballet, brain, it's gym today!'"

"Oh, well. It won't be for long," said Poppy, grabbing my hand. "Come on, I'll help you with *jetés*."

Poppy and Jasmine are dying for my gym competition to be over because they both know I'll never be in their ballet class with them until I've passed grade four. And that's not going to happen until I stop getting ballet mixed up with gym.

We'd only just started on the *jetés* when Miss Banner, the gym teacher, appeared at the playground gate, with her portable CD player in one hand and her bag in the other.

Poppy gave me an accusing look, as though I'd specially invited Miss Banner today. "*She* doesn't usually come on Wednesdays!"

"Extra practice." I sighed.

"But that'll make three times this week!" squeaked Poppy.

"Four, actually."

"Four! But you only do ballet *once*! It's no wonder you keep over arching and everything." Poppy had gone a little pink. She'd probably just realized how bossy she was sounding.

Miss Banner spotted me and came jogging over. "Make sure you're in the hall at one o'clock sharp, Rose. And can you tell Sasha and Katie?"

There must have been a little fed-upness still left on my face because Miss Banner was just turning to go when she suddenly gave me a knowing-teacher look. "Gymnasts don't get anywhere without hard work, you know, Rose. Anyway, I thought you loved gym..."

I wasn't sure what to say to that and decided it might be best to keep quiet in case something came out that sounded sassy by mistake. Sometimes it's hard to judge the right things to say to teachers. At least, it is for *me*.

"Good, Rose... And get ready for your run up..."

The energy came swishing up my legs and zooming into my chest. Miss Banner watched me as I set off toward the vault like a plane going down a runway, getting faster and faster. I bounced off the springboard and slapped my hands onto the middle of the vault, felt my legs fling up as my back arched and I flew into my handspring. A second later, I was on the crash mattress, feet together, legs stretched, back arched even more, and my head flung back.

"Lovely presentation at the end there, Rose, and nice flight off and landing, but the attack to the vault was a bit weak, and that's because you're not giving it enough oomph. You've got to forget about being gentle and balletic and really go for it."

Not enough oomph? How much oomph did she want? "I ran as hard as I could...I thought I was the oomphiest person on the planet, to be honest."

Miss Banner was staring at me as though I was speaking another language or something. "But you were running like a ballet dancer, far too high up on the balls of your feet. I don't know how I'm going to get you out of the habit..." She didn't even finish her sentence, just shook her head and then turned to Sasha and Katie, who were both looking at the floor.

"Right, let's go through the floor-work routine to finish."

We all went to our starting positions on the thin mats and Miss Banner watched the three of us carefully as we stayed still as statues.

"Lovely, Sasha... Can you drop your head a little more, Katie...?" She pointed the remote at the CD player and the music started. "And *five* and *six* and *seven* and *eight* and..."

It was a three-minute routine and we know it really well because we've practiced so much. I felt strong and full of energy as I went in and out of rolls and springs, twists and jumps, balances and stretches. Miss Banner didn't say a word until the music had finished and we were holding our final shapes.

"Great! It's really coming together." She turned to me with a smile that was a sort of apology for what she'd said earlier. "This is where ballet can be helpful, and you've certainly got a lovely dance quality to your floor work now, but your arms are rather curvy and soft. I just wish I could sharpen you up a little..." She suddenly stood up straight in the middle of the mat, her arms in ballet fifth position. "Look, Rose." She purposely bent her elbows too much and drooped her wrists so her fingers dangled. "That's ballet!" Then she straightened her arms into a wide straight V-shape with fingers neatly together. "And *that's* gym!"

I tried to keep my face blank even though I really would have liked to stick my tongue out at her. I hate it when teachers exaggerate, especially as you aren't allowed to argue with them and you just have to wait until they've finished.

"One more time through, then we'll call it a day, girls."

This time I concentrated hard and when it got to the middle part I stretched my arms like crazy.

"Much better!" said Miss Banner at the end. Her eyes were sparkling.

"Well done," whispered Katie, as she and Sasha rushed off to get changed.

I was about to follow them but Miss Banner called me over.

"I've had details today about a big competition later in the year for solo entries and I'd like to enter you, Rose." She patted my shoulder. "It'll take extra training, but I'll have a word with your mom about my Saturday-afternoon class."

Lots of jumbled thoughts whizzed around my head.

Miss Banner has chosen me to compete in a big competition. Yesss! – But I'd have to go to gym class on Saturday afternoons when I really want to be with Jasmine and Poppy. – I'd get better and better at gym and make everyone really proud of me. – Yes, but I'd get worse and worse at ballet. – No, I could try harder and harder at ballet. – But Miss Coralie would still be able to tell I was doing lots of gym. She's already noticed. She'd say that gym and ballet don't mix. – I've found that out already. – I'd have to give one of them up. – I don't want to. – I'd have to. – I don't want to. – I'd...

None of the thoughts would stay still for long enough to turn into a real sentence that I could actually say to Miss Banner. But she was waiting for me to say *something*. Her eyes were staring so hard that I began to think she might have some special powers to see inside my head and any second now she'd let me have it for wanting to do ballet just as much as I wanted to do gym. Then, suddenly, her whole face broke into a smile and she said, "One thing at a time, though. Let's get *this* competition over with first, shall we?"

I nodded, feeling relieved that I didn't have to speak after all. All I wanted was to get back to Poppy. With a little luck there might still be a few minutes of recess before the bell. "See you tomorrow, Miss Banner."

"See you tomorrow, Rose." I was almost out the door when she added, "And don't forget to bring plenty of *oomph* with you!"

I gulped. I wished there was no such word as *oomph*. In fact, I wished there was no such word as competition. I used to love them... But I don't know what's the matter with me now.

3 Gran

On Sunday, Gran came around for lunch. She wanted to know all the details about the gym competition.

"A very important date for my diary, dear!"

Then Mom said lunch wouldn't be ready for twenty minutes, so I grabbed Gran's hand.

"Do you want to watch me do ballet, or shall we go outside and I'll show you some of the floor work for the gym competition?"

"Now, you be careful, Rose," said Mom, waving a cloth at me from the kitchen door. "Don't do anything that might strain your muscles, or you'll have Miss Banner up in arms."

"It'll be okay so long as I don't do handsprings and stuff."

"Probably better not to take any risks as you've got the competition coming up," said Gran, patting my hand. "Come on, let's go to your room."

I was already wearing my ballet leotard because Poppy and Jazz were coming around after lunch. They were going to help me with the set variations. I couldn't wait.

"It's taking you a long time to grow into this leotard of yours, isn't it?" said Gran as we reached the top of the stairs.

"I reckon it'd fit *you*, Gran!" said my brother, Adam, suddenly appearing in his bedroom doorway.

"Too much cheek by far, for an eleven year old!" joked Gran.

Adam just grinned and whizzed downstairs. Gran never does real tellings off.

✳

At lunchtime, Dad told everyone what Miss Banner had said when she phoned about the big competition.

He winked at me and I felt very proud. "She thinks you're the bee's knees!"

Mom suddenly started flapping her hand in the air. "Yes! And I forgot to tell you, Rose, Miss Banner wants you to do more classes. She's not even going to charge us, and she says she's going to figure out a daily practice routine for you centered around body conditioning!" She leaned forward with sparkling eyes. "What do you think of *that*?"

It was happening again. The thoughts were whizzing around inside my head but none of them would stay still. So I just shrugged, and said, "I don't know."

"I thought you'd be over the moon," said Mom, frowning. "Miss Banner sounded very excited, you know."

I stabbed a piece of pork chop and skated it around my plate on the end of my fork. "She gets angry sometimes."

"What for?" said Jack. (He's fifteen, by the way.)

"When I get confused with ballet..."

"You should give up ballet. It's for wimps," said Rory, my thirteen-year-old brother.

"Don't talk with your mouth full," said Mom. She was staring at the peas really hard, then she suddenly gave me a gentle look. "You can always give up ballet until the gym competition's over if you want, honey."

But that wasn't what I wanted. "No, I don't want to miss any ballet. Except..."

Gran tipped her head on one side. "What's up, dear?"

"It's just that Miss Coralie gets a little fed up, too. She says I keep dancing like a gymnast."

Dad started stabbing the air with his fork. "Somebody should tell Miss Coralie that the reason you dance like a gymnast is because you *are* one!"

I didn't like to hear Dad getting angry with Miss Coralie. He didn't understand. "She's only telling the truth, Dad. If you do lots of gym, it really *is* bad for ballet, honestly."

"What garbage," said Dad, leaning back in his chair and folding his arms.

"Why don't you give up gym then?" said Adam. "Can I have some more fries, Mom?"

Mom nodded. "Rose wouldn't dream of giving up gym, would you, Rose?" She didn't wait for an answer. "Miss Banner said she's the best in the school at it. And you can't go giving up something when you've got a real talent for it, can you?"

"How come *ballet's* bad for *gym*?" asked Jack.

"It just is," I said, remembering how Miss Banner had stood in the middle of the mats with dangling arms.

"So give up ballet, like I said. *Duh!*" said Rory.

Suddenly, I'd had enough of the whole conversation. Everyone thought they knew all the answers, but there weren't any answers. I just wished they'd all shut up. "Can I leave the table please, Mom?"

"You've not had any dessert, honey."

"I'm not really hungry."

"Go on, then." I could feel her eyes on me as I went toward the kitchen.

"Going to practice ballet, I bet," called Adam. Then he put on the snobby voice he uses when he's pretending to be my ballet teacher. "Point those toes, now Rosie Pose!"

Everyone laughed. At least, I think they did. I didn't stop to check, just ran down the back steps and onto the lawn. The grass was a little damp, but that never bothers me. I kicked off my sneakers, pulled off my socks, put my hand on the side of the old swing and started doing *pliés*. I could hear the *plié* music in my head, almost as though Mrs. Marsden was playing it. But when I went on to *battements tendus*, I couldn't remember the music at all, so my head started filling up with the conversation we'd just had. It made me mad that everyone seemed to think ballet wasn't anything important. They should go to lessons, then they'd find out.

"That's a fierce face!" I looked sideways and saw Gran coming down the back steps. I was glad it was her and not anyone else in my stupid family. "Sorry, dear. I didn't mean to interrupt your *battements tendus*. I just thought you looked a little upset when you came out here."

"I hate it when everyone says stuff about ballet."

Gran sat on the swing and started swinging gently back and forth. I noticed how straight her back was. And when she stretched her legs out at the front, they were straight too. I don't think many grandmothers would have such lovely, strong, upright bodies as that. Most ladies go a little humpy and lumpy when they get old.

"They don't understand how much you like it, dear. I would just ignore them."

"But I can't ignore Miss Coralie and Miss Banner, can I? I'm sick of getting told off when it's not my fault."

"They're not exactly telling you off, are they? Just trying to make you better at the thing they teach."

I didn't know what to say after that, because Gran was right, but it still left an enormous problem inside my head. I stared at the ground and found my foot doing *ronds de jambe* without me telling it to.

"When I was your age," Gran started to say, in a slow, dreamy voice, "I felt as though I could see my whole life ahead of me, like a long, straight, smooth-flowing river..." She was looking at the sky with an almost-smile on her face. I stopped doing *ronds de jambe* so I could listen better, because I had the feeling Gran was about to tell me something important. A very thoughtful look came over her face. "It wasn't till I was seventeen that I realized something about rivers, though. You see..." She stopped right in the middle of her sentence because we'd both heard a loud knocking on the window. I looked up to see Dad mouthing that Poppy and Jasmine were here.

"Ooh, lovely. Now you can all practice dancing together!" said Gran.

"They're going to teach me the grade four set variations!"

"That'll be good. You'll have to show me afterward."

Then Poppy and Jasmine were standing at the back door, Jasmine in third position and Poppy with her head tilted, which made her neck look really graceful.

"Go and dance your heart out!" called Gran as I rushed off.

But the moment we were up in my room, I burst into a flood of talking and talking about

Miss Banner and Miss Coralie and how impossible it was to be a gymnast *and* do ballet.

"Miss Banner must think you're brilliant, Rose!" said Jasmine, when I was in the middle of the part about all the extra gym practices. "She might be thinking that you could represent the country one day! Think how good that would be!"

"But I'd have to give up ballet!" I said in a kind of a squeak, because I couldn't believe that Jasmine seemed to be agreeing with Mom and Dad, when I thought she was my ballet friend.

"I'm sure it'll be all right to keep doing both..." said Poppy. "I can't wait to see you in the competition."

"I can't wait to see *myself*!"I said, which made them both burst out laughing. "But what's going to happen afterward? I mean, just imagine if we couldn't get together on Saturday afternoons because I had to do more gym practice!"

"We'd just have to do ballet on Sundays instead – like right now!" said Poppy.

They were both talking as though it was no problem at all, but there was something not completely right. And then I realized what it was. Their eyes seemed worried and they wouldn't look at me. So what was I supposed to believe, their eyes or their voices? And will someone please tell me why there are so many unanswered questions racing around inside my head these days?

"Come on, let's get on with it!" said Jasmine. "I'll be Miss Coralie..." She'd already taken off her leggings and top and was wearing her leotard underneath. "Good afternoon, girls..." Poppy quickly took off her jeans so she was ready too, and stood by my windowsill, which we use for a *barre*.

Any second now Jasmine would say, "First position and prepare the arm to second..." just like Miss Coralie does, so I quickly rushed over to my desk and sat down.

"Rose! What are you doing!" said Jasmine, forgetting who she was supposed to be for a moment.

"I'm being Mrs. Marsden," I told her. "I mean, *someone's* got to be the pianist, haven't they?"

Poppy was laughing too much to stand up straight. "You're insane, Rose!"

And she was right, I *am* a bit crazy. But these days, it's only the top layer. Underneath, I'm deadly serious and all confused. Especially now my best friends don't even know the answer to my problem.

4 Time to Make a Decision

It wasn't until I was lying in bed that night that I remembered how Gran had been just about to tell me something when Poppy and Jasmine had arrived. It had sounded as though it was going to be important and suddenly I just *had* to know what it was that Gran had found out when she was seventeen. I don't know why, but I thought it might help me figure things out in my own life.

The first thing I did the next morning was ask Mom if I could go around to Gran's after school, but she told me that Gran was going to stay with Uncle Rupert until Thursday. I felt a little sad about that. Thursday was three whole days away.

Monday night's homework was awful and I didn't really understand what it was about so I asked if I could call Jazz. She'd be sure to know the answers. But first she wanted to know how my gym class had gone.

I told her it was okay – "Well, the second half was. For the first half, Miss Banner told me I was too dreamy."

A big gasp came down the line. *"You! Dreamy!"*

"I know!"

"Maybe she meant *day*dreamy, not the gentle floaty kind of dreamy."

"No, she definitely meant the gentle floaty kind. It made me really mad so after that I turned into the opposite of dreamy and went all hard and sharp."

There was a silence when I said that. I knew what Jazz was thinking – that she didn't want me to be *too* hard and sharp or Miss Coralie would get angry with me. I couldn't be bothered to go through all that again so I asked her about the homework and by the time we'd finished I had to get off the phone because Dad said I'd been on long enough.

After I'd done the homework, I started thinking about ballet, and I felt really determined to get a *lovely* in the lesson the next day. So I decided to get gym right out of my body by shaking myself hard, and kicking my feet. But after only a minute Dad came up and said that the ceiling was trembling in the den, and that whatever I was doing had to stop.

All through Tuesday at school I got more and more nervous – the excited sort of nervous – and by the time we all ran in at the start of Miss Coralie's lesson, and found our places on the *barre*, I couldn't wait to get started. Miss Coralie didn't really notice my *pliés* because she was correcting some of the girls at the other end of the *barre*, but when it came to *ronds de jambe* she was standing right next to me.

"Your placing's gone completely haywire, Rose. Lower that hip."

She might as well have poked me in the stomach and said *I hate you*, the way she made me feel at that moment. I'd been so sure I was all lined up correctly. I lowered my hip as carefully as I could, but I could still feel my leg turning in.

"Dear, oh dear!" She bent down and altered my leg and foot. "What's happened to your turnout?" She straightened up. "That's better... But I shouldn't have to remind you every five minutes." I was annoyed with myself then, because I should have realized my placing was wrong.

I concentrated as hard as I could right to the end of the *barre* work, and all that time I could feel Miss Coralie's eyes on me. Then we moved to the center and still her eyes seemed to be on me more than on anyone else. We were right in the middle of the *port de bras* when she suddenly said, "Arms, Rose!" I quickly snapped them into a strong, straight V and arched my back at the same time.

Why had one of the girls behind me gasped? And why was Miss Coralie looking so stern? Then I realized where I was. At ballet. Not gym. Oh, no! My arms immediately bent like thin branches snapping, as my heart somersaulted down to my stomach.

"What *are* you doing, Rose?"

"Sorry, I got confused."

The music for the exercise had finished now and it seemed very quiet. Mrs. Marsden was looking down at her hands in her lap. The girls in the row in front had all turned round to stare at me. If I'd been anywhere but here I would have made a face and asked them if they wanted a picture. But I just stood there, keeping my face blank.

"Let's move on to the *adage*, girls."

And that was it. Everyone faced the right way for the next exercise, Mrs. Marsden's eyes went back to her music, my heart went back into its place and the lesson carried on as normal. But I didn't enjoy it at all because I had to keep giving myself instructions all the time, like: *Bend your arms, Rose! Don't arch your back, Rose! Turn OUT, Rose! Don't be so sharp, Rose!* It was a relief when we got to the *révérence*. Then, I was about to go out to the changing room with everyone else when Miss Coralie called me back.

"Rose, I want a word with you about gym. Are you doing more than usual at the moment?"

"Well, yes, there's another competition, you see... But it'll soon be over."

She gave me one of her half-smiles. I felt as though I'd scored five out of ten with that answer. Then I couldn't help watching her lips to see what score I'd get for the next one.

"I see. So when the competition's over, you'll be going back to what? A weekly gym lesson?"

The trouble was, Mom really wanted me to take the Saturday afternoon class. "Erm...I'm not really sure..."

Well *that* scored me about two, I guess.

"You love gymnastics, don't you?"

Easy question. I nodded and waited for her lips to move, but they didn't. Her eyes had turned even more serious, with a hint of sadness in them. "You're lovely and flexible, Rose, and that's probably largely because of all your gym... I should imagine you're a very talented gymnast, and it's no wonder your teacher is urging you to enter competitions and get plenty of practice and so on... But all the time you're doing *this* amount of gym, you're not going to get anywhere with ballet. It affects your placing so much..." Her eyes had gotten softness in them now, which was spreading all over her face. I'd never ever seen that before in Miss Coralie. "When you first started ballet I didn't realize you'd be doing *so* much gym, or I'd have explained that the two don't really mix. Maybe it's time to make a decision about whether you're going to concentrate on ballet or gym."

There was a long pause. I suppose we'd come to the end of the conversation. I didn't know what the right answer was, so I just stood there.

"Take some time and think it over. Talk to your parents. Ask them to call me if they want. I'll be very happy to discuss it with them."

Her smile grew a little bigger, but it was only to get rid of me. So I nodded and ran out of the room as she called out, "Come in, class."

Poppy and Jasmine were giving me big-eyed looks from the line.

"What?" asked Jasmine in a squeaky whisper.

I shook my head because there wasn't time to talk, and they both came out of the line to press their thumbs against mine. We call it a thumb-thumb and it's usually for luck, but this time it was just because they felt sorry for me.

"I'll call you later," I said.

But I didn't really know what good it would do, because Poppy and Jasmine don't do gym. How could they possibly understand that if I gave it up I'd be giving up half my life, and if I gave up ballet, I'd be giving up the other half?

5 The Wrong Kind of Audience

In the car on the way home I kept *nearly* telling Mom what Miss Coralie had said. But I couldn't think of the right words because I knew Mom would get angry and say she didn't see why I shouldn't do both. Then *I'd* get angry back trying to explain that they don't mix at all. And that would be the end of that.

If I talked to Dad about it, he'd probably just tell me to give up ballet. And I didn't want to. I couldn't ask any of my brothers what they thought I should do because they weren't really interested in anything I did. Poppy and Jasmine would both want to me to give up gym, only they'd be too nice to say that, because they know I love it. So there was no one left for me to talk to except Gran, and she wouldn't be back till Thursday.

While Mom made the tea, I sat at the kitchen table reading my *World of Ballet* book. Really, I was only turning the pages and looking at the pictures. It was just that I wanted to be in the same room as Mom in case I suddenly found the right words to explain about ballet and gym, because I'd figured out that it was going to be forty-eight whole hours before I could see Gran, and that was a very long time. Anyway, it was cozy in the kitchen.

But then Adam came in and spoiled it. "Rory's swiped my soccer socks. He says they're his, but they're not, are they, Mom?"

Mom yanked open the clothes dryer, pulled out a pair of socks and threw them to Adam. "There you go. Figure it out between yourselves."

Adam caught them, then looked at me. "What are you doing?"

"Nothing."

"Why are you all quiet?"

"I'm not."

"What are you reading?" He looked at the cover and put on his sneery voice. "*World of Ballet*. Has it got Miss Coronary in it?" He snickered.

"*Coralie!*" I snapped.

"When's dinner, Mom?"

"Fifteen minutes."

"Can I have a cookie?"

"No."

"Some raisins?"

"All right, go on."

Adam helped himself to a handful of raisins and came and sat at the table with me to eat them. I put the book up to hide his face from my view. Then he stood up and started to imitate the dancer on the front cover who was in an *arabesque*. "Is this right?"

I snapped the book shut, trying hard to keep my anger inside me, and said I was going outside.

"To dance on your tippy toes," said Adam in a whisper so Mom wouldn't hear.

"No, gym actually!" I only said that because Adam thinks I'm pretty cool to be able to do half the gym things I do.

"Bet you're not doing gym," he said.

I didn't bother to answer him, just went out. As I was shutting the door behind me, I heard Mom letting him have it for teasing me. At least I knew then that it would be safe to do ballet, even though it was right outside the kitchen window, because Mom would stop Adam from watching me. It had been raining and the grass was wet, but I still took my socks and sneakers off so I could point my toes correctly.

As I slowly practiced my *ronds de jambe*, I found myself filling up with even more determination to get a *lovely* from Miss Coralie, even though it was only about an hour since I'd been thinking it would be impossible *ever* to get one. I tried to imagine Miss Coralie's eyes on me, and made myself keep my hips square. I couldn't stop my working leg turning in when I slid my toe around to the back, though.

Suddenly there was a knock on an upstairs window and, like an idiot, I looked up. Adam opened Rory's window, stuck his leg on the windowsill and then put his arms above his head like Miss Banner had done.

I should have just ignored him and kept going, but it's hard doing ballet practice with anyone watching because it's private. It's got feelings in it and you have to make the feelings come out. That's fine when I'm in a class with *everyone* showing their feelings, but you feel kind of stupid when you're the only one. It would be much easier to just pretend I was doing exercises for gym. So I quickly changed from *ronds de jambe* to the sideways splits.

"Doesn't that hurt?" asked Rory, appearing next to Adam at the window.

I felt very superior having both of them watch me and knowing that neither of them could do anything like that, so I did a handstand and walked a few steps. But it made me feel guilty because I was doing something I wasn't supposed to do. Miss Banner was always giving us lectures about practicing at home and how easy it is to strain wrists and ankles, so I came down from the handstand.

"Hey, she's good, your sister!"

I looked up at the sound of the strange voice to see one of Rory's friends at the window.

"Show us one of those round-off things," said Rory.

"I'm not really allowed," I said, shrugging my shoulders to show it wasn't me who made up the rules. "I could twist my ankle or something. And I've got the competition..."

"Anyway, what *is* a round-off?" asked Rory's friend.

"Just do one, Ro...to show Jonno. Go on... You're really good at them."

It was such a good feeling hearing Rory saying nice things when I'm used to nothing but teasing, but still I wasn't sure.

"It'll be good practice for the competition," said Jonno.

He was right. It would. And just one wouldn't do any harm, would it? So I went to the top of the garden to get the longest possible run up.

But then Adam suddenly spoke in his I-know-best voice. "You're supposed to warm up first, you know."

"I *am* warmed up," I told him. I couldn't help snapping because I'd been just about to start and he'd interrupted my concentration.

"Well, don't blame me if you get injured," he said, making his voice go all grown-up and know-it-all.

I glanced at the kitchen window to make sure Mom wasn't watching. There was no sign of her, so I set off, pounding the ground with my hard steps. It felt easy because it was slightly downhill, and when I sprung off my hands, my legs flung over really fast and the ground seemed to come up to meet my feet before I was expecting it. I had to do a little jump to stop myself crashing forward. And it was then that I felt a pain like a hot knife cutting into the top of my right foot.

6 Dreading the Next Day

Rory and Jonno both whistled and whooped as they turned away. Adam was the only one there now. I could feel his eyes on me. My foot was in agony but there was no way I was going to let smarty pants know that. I carefully sat down on the ground, put my legs in a wide V and did some stretches over my legs. My foot didn't hurt in this position, thank goodness, so I knew I could keep doing them for as long as I wanted.

"You've hurt yourself, haven't you?" came Adam's I'm-so-clever voice. "I can tell. It's because you didn't warm up, isn't it?"

How could he tell, the big creep? And anyway it wasn't because of not warming up enough, it was because of the ground sloping.

"I haven't hurt myself at all. I don't know what you're talking about," I told him.

I was wishing I hadn't sat down, because that meant I had to stand up again, and I knew it was going to hurt. Maybe if I tried kneeling first. So I carefully got onto my knees without putting any pressure on my foot, and started doing some sideways stretches.

Hurry up and go, Adam!

"If it doesn't hurt, let's see you stand up, then!" he said, all sneery.

"I will...when I've done this." And I changed to head rolls so I could keep an eye on the upstairs window. Every time I looked, the big know-it-all was still there. It was obvious he was waiting to catch me out, and if I did even the tiniest wince he'd say, *See! Told you! You* have *injured yourself!*

And it was right at that moment that it hit me. *I HAD injured myself.* I might not be able to do the competition. After all that work, I'd be letting everyone down. Especially me. And as for Miss Banner, she'd go totally berserk. And so would Miss Coralie. *And* Mom and Dad. But why was I thinking about Adam? Who cared about Adam? Except that if he saw me limping he'd probably tell Mom right away, and then the whole big horrible fuss would start. I felt awful. All I wanted was to be on my own so I could wiggle my foot around and try rubbing it and see how bad it was. But I couldn't do anything except silly head rolls because of hawk eyes watching me all the time.

If only I hadn't been such a show-off. No wonder Miss Banner doesn't like people trying out their skills at home. Anyway, I couldn't do head rolls forever. I had to stand up. Okay... slowly and carefully...

"See! Your ankle's hurting, isn't it?"

I didn't have to tell a lie. It was nothing to do with my ankle. "No it's not, know-all! I'm just going slowly because that's what you're supposed to do. It's all part of the stretching."

I put my weight on my right foot. It *did* hurt, but it wasn't agony. I could easily pretend it was perfectly all right just till I got back inside the house.

Adam was pointing at me by now. "You're faking it! I'll tell Mom. She'll know what to do."

He was just trying to trick me. He wanted me to say: *No, please don't tell!*

But all I said was "I'm okay, *okay*?"

"Do a handstand, then. You're allowed to do ordinary handstands, aren't you?"

So I did, and as I came down I felt that same stabbing pain, but I managed not to flinch or anything, just stood there, looking up. "There! Satisfied?"

"You were lucky," was all he said. Then he slammed shut the window.

The moment he was gone I put my socks and sneakers back on. Then, when I was sure no one was watching from any of the windows, I tested out my right foot by walking slowly toward the back door. If I stepped very gently, and took care that my foot was facing exactly forward, it didn't hurt at all, but if I put it down quickly and it was pointing even slightly in the wrong direction it really hurt.

By the time I got to the back door I was beginning to worry about how I was going to hide it from everyone. The whole family was used to seeing me darting around all over the place. They'd know something was wrong if I suddenly started going around like a turtle.

And when I thought about gym practice the next day...I just had to shake the thought away because I had no idea what in the world I was going to say to Miss Banner. All I knew was that it wouldn't be the truth or she'd kill me.

"Dinner's ready." Luckily, Mom wasn't

looking at me, she was stirring something in a pan. "Can you go and wash your hands, Rose, and tell the boys to come down and set the table?"

I walked slowly across the kitchen and had nearly reached the hall door when Mom said, "What's the matter with your foot?"

"Nothing. It's just...a floor exercise Miss Banner said I should do. You walk very slowly and try to let your whole foot spread out. But it's important that you keep your feet pointing exactly forward."

I don't know where on earth my brain managed to find that answer, but it sounded just like the truth.

"Uh-huh..." said Mom in the murmury voice that meant she was concentrating on something completely different. Then she suddenly went bright and brisk again. "Oh, Gran called and she's coming back tomorrow instead of Thursday."

A big zing of happiness went right through my body. At last something good had happened. "Can I go and see her after school then?"

"I think so." Mom smiled.

I smiled too. Only one more day, then Gran would talk to me in her lovely Gran voice and help me sort out all the jumble inside my head. And she'd never be angry with me for getting hurt.

But right in the middle of my lovely thoughts the big shivery thought came back. Before I saw Gran, I had to get through school. It was going to be like a terrible nightmare. Just a horrible day of faking and pretending and lying. Unless, by some miracle, my foot got better overnight. I knew that resting injured parts of your body does them good. Okay, so I'd hop everywhere so long as no one was watching, then I'd go to bed early so it could rest for the longest possible time.

I sighed as I turned around to go upstairs on

my bottom. Somehow, I didn't think it was going to work. If only Poppy and Jasmine were here to do a thumb-thumb...

7 Everything Coming to the Surface

"What am I going to do, Poppy?" I asked her for the trillionth time.

"Just try wiggling it. See if it's gotten any better in the last five minutes. It might have, you never know."

"I spent hours wiggling it in bed last night, and that didn't do any good, so I don't think it's going to make much difference now."

A thoughtful look came over Poppy's face and she spoke slowly, staring at the far wall of the playground. "Perhaps you should tell Miss Banner the truth."

"What! You're joking!"

"No, listen. Miss Banner might know something to put on it...or some special exercises that you can do...or something."

"It's a good idea, Poppy, except that I really don't want to get killed for breaking the rules. I'm too young to die."

Poppy wasn't in the mood for my jokes. Neither was *I* really. "No, you don't have to tell the *whole* truth. You could say you did it falling downstairs or you tripped over something."

I shook my head. "Miss Banner knows everything about muscles and all those little – what d'you call them – ligaments and things. She'd guess I was lying because it's probably impossible to get an injury on the top of your foot from falling downstairs."

"So what *are* you going to do then?"

While Poppy had been talking about falling downstairs, a plan had been coming into my brain.

I spoke slowly to test it out. "What if...I pretended...to be...sick?"

"They'd send you home, and your Mom'd know right away that you weren't really!" Poppy said in a rush.

"Okay, not really sick...more....kind of tired..."

Poppy didn't say anything, so I told her to put her arm around me, then I made my shoulders go all droopy. "Try to look as though you're worried about me."

And sure enough, when we'd stayed like that for a minute or two, the teacher came over.

"Are you all right, Rose?"

"I feel kind of funny – kind of tired..."

And by one o'clock, all the teachers, including Miss Banner, thought it was best not to exhaust me by making me do gym practice.

"Better to miss one practice and get yourself back on form," said Miss Banner, tilting my chin back to look closely at me. It reminded me of when Mom searches Jack's face for blackheads. "Let's see how you are tomorrow. I'm sure you'll be fine."

I nodded and tried to make sure I kept my droopy look in place. Then I walked slowly away, being careful to take only footsteps that faced forward.

A little voice inside me was whispering, *What if it isn't better by tomorrow? Or even worse, what if it isn't better in time for the competition?* But I decided to ignore that voice and just hope for the best.

At the end of school, Mrs. Henderson, my class teacher, talked to Mom and explained about me being tired.

"Tired? Well she's not short of sleep..." said Mom.

"No, I think it's just all the gym practice that's suddenly gotten to her. It's understandable."

Mom was frowning at me as though she didn't think it was at all understandable.

I leaned my head into her and she put her arm around me, looking totally puzzled. "Come on then, dear. Let's get you home."

Then I wished I hadn't leaned into her because now I had to get out from under her arm. Otherwise, I wouldn't be able to walk with my feet facing forward and it still hurt like crazy when I put my right foot down wrong.

"I *can* still go to Gran's, can't I?" I asked, the moment we set off.

"So you don't feel too tired to go to Gran's?" She didn't exactly sound angry, just puzzled.

"It doesn't make me tired to be at Gran's. We just talk."

Mom looked as though she was thinking hard, but then all the thoughts came pouring out in a rush.

"You see, I'm not sure what's wrong with you, Rose. I've never known you feel tired for no reason before. I mean...what kind of tiredness is it? Do your eyes feel sleepy? Or does your body feel tired, or what?"

I knew I had to be careful. The teachers had believed me completely but it wasn't so easy to fool Mom. "Body," I said.

She seemed to ignore that. "Or is there a reason why you didn't want to go to gym? Because if there is, you only have to tell me, dear."

She turned her head sideways and the look on her face reminded me of when I was only about five and I'd eaten some ice cream straight from the tub in the freezer without asking, and Mom was trying to get me to admit it.

"I just felt too tired to do all those hard things again," I said, heaving a big sigh.

Mom patted my knee and we drove the rest of the way in a thoughtful silence.

At six-thirty, I was sitting in the big armchair at Gran's, which has got its own special smell.

I was balancing a plate of cookies on my lap.
Well, to be exact, I was whizzing them around to
see how fast they'd spin without falling off,
because they were very thin shiny, slippery ones.
Gran said she'd gotten them from Uncle Rupert.

"Did you have a nice time at Great Uncle
Rupert's?"

"Wonderful! We've been reminiscing."

"What's that?"

"Talking about the old days...and looking at
photos from when we were both young."

"Ooh, can I look? Are there any of when you
used to do ballet?"

She pointed toward the sideboard. "Bring me
over those albums, dear. I got them out just
before you came."

I remembered to walk carefully.

"Rose, what have you done to your foot?"

I couldn't help a gasp coming out. "How did
you know?"

"Because I know my granddaughter, and she

doesn't walk like a snail unless there's something wrong with her." She gave another chuckle. "Show me where it hurts and I'll see what I can do!"

I put the albums on the coffee table, then sat down with my foot on Gran's lap. "It's just here." I pressed the place, which was in a fleshy hollow part on top but not right in the middle. "Ouch!"

"Yes, I see..." She lent forward and touched it herself. "Does that hurt?"

I nodded.

"How did you do it?"

I told her the truth right away and she wasn't at all angry. Just said, "That'll be a tendon. We'll see what we can do with that."

But, as Gran started to massage my foot, I noticed what it said on the front cover of the photograph album: *Me – 14 to 17*. Then I spotted something else right at the bottom of the cover. Someone had cut out a picture of a ballet shoe and stuck it in the corner.

"Are these photos of you doing ballet, Gran? Did you do it until you were seventeen? I didn't know that!" I sat up and took my foot off her lap. Then I realized Gran wasn't answering. I turned to look at her. She was smiling with twinkling secretive eyes. And suddenly I knew... I snatched up the album and turned to the first page. Then I gasped and held my breath as I stared and stared at the beautiful photo.

She was wearing a leotard and a little ballet skirt, standing on *pointe*, in the most perfect *arabesque*, like a real ballerina.

"Wow! You were amazing!" I breathed.

And when I looked up, I saw that Gran had tears in her eyes.

8 The River

The album was full of photos of Gran doing ballet. Every single one made shivers go up my arms. I couldn't speak. I just wanted to keep staring and staring – Gran in a *plié* with the most perfect turnout in the world; Gran bending down to tie up her shoe with the straightest back in the world; Gran standing on *pointe* with the best arch I've ever seen. *My* Gran. Doing ballet, just like I do, except about a million times better.

Then we came to the very last photo in the book. It took up nearly the whole page. Gran was wearing a long white ballet dress, her hair really scraped back with a little silver headdress, and she had make-up on. It was a beautiful picture and I couldn't take my eyes off it.

"I gave up shortly after that," she said in a quiet voice.

"But why? You must have been brilliant at it. Why did you give up?"

"I wasn't brilliant, dear. *Good*, I'll grant you. But not brilliant. And there were girls out there who were better than I was. It was as simple as that. I knew in my heart that I'd never be good enough to be a ballerina. So I gave up."

"Oh, Gran. That's terrible. I bet you *could* have been a ballerina."

She didn't say anything, but I could still see tears in her eyes and I think they were new ones.

"*I* love ballet too," I told her, to cheer her up. "I'm really glad you gave me that present."

"I thought you would. That's why I wanted you to try it."

"But how could you tell I'd like it? Was it because I was good at gym?"

"No, it was just because you reminded me of *me* so much. I used to go careering around at top speed, just like you, always chasing after things and never stopping to smell the roses..."

"Smell the roses?"

"It's an expression. It means never appreciating the things around you. I thought ballet was stupid when I was about eight. I even teased some of the girls at school who did it. But then one day we went to a play – *Jack and the Beanstalk* it was – and there was a scene with some ballet dancing. The dancers were supposed to be the sylphs of the clouds, and my brothers were huffing and puffing and scowling and muttering because they wanted to get to the part where the giant appeared. And I started imitating them like I always did. But then I realized that I was enjoying watching the dancing. And gradually as it went on, I got more and more excited about it. And the very second the curtain went down for the intermission I started begging to be allowed to go to ballet classes. It took me nearly a year of pestering to get them."

"Wow!" I breathed. Then I didn't feel like saying anything at all for a while. I just wanted to think about all that Gran had told me, and try to imagine what it must have been like. So we went through the album again, only backward this time, and when we were on the very first page I decided to tell Gran what had happened at the last ballet lesson.

"Miss Coralie says that all the extra gym I'm doing is having a bad effect on my ballet and I've got to make a decision about whether I'm going to concentrate on ballet or gym. But how can I choose when I love them both? You see, I keep thinking I'm in gym when I'm really in ballet and then I think I'm in ballet when I'm at gym. And it makes me do things all wrong. So I make stiff, straight arms for ballet and forget to turn out, and then I use soft arms for gym and run too gently and things like that, and both teachers get angry with me, but how am I supposed to remember what I'm doing? It's impossible to always get it right and..."

I could feel a lump in my throat but I never ever cry so I tried to swallow it down. But Gran put her arm around me and said, "Ssh, it's all right, dear," into my hair and then I couldn't stop the tears coming out of my eyes, and next minute I was really crying and crying.

I tried to tell her that I'm not normally such a baby, but she just kept shushing me and saying that crying's good for you, and even boys sometimes do it in private. So in the end I gave in, and sobbed great big sobs, but it didn't matter.

Then, just when I was blowing my nose, the phone rang and it was Mom wanting me to go back home, but Gran asked Mom if I could stay the night and I could tell what Mom was saying on the other end because of Gran's answers.

"No, she can use her finger to clean her teeth just this once... No, don't worry about bringing anything over, I'm sure I can find her something to sleep in... All right, dear. I'll walk her around at eight-thirty when she's had her breakfast... Yes, dear... Yes, I'll make sure she's in bed early... She's just sitting quietly with me and we're having a chat... Yes... All right, dear, bye bye."

I was so happy about staying the night. Now I'd have tons of time to talk to Gran. I smiled at her through my tears, then she went to get me a paper towel to wipe my face.

"That's better, isn't it?"

I nodded and did one of those sobby sighs that goes upward.

"Right. First things first." She sat down on the couch and told me to put my foot back on her lap. "This is the place, right?"

I nodded.

"We need to massage it gently in tiny circles and I think that should work. I reckon this is the same injury that I had when I was fifteen and about to take a ballet exam. It was a physiotherapist who taught me how to massage across the tendons like this." Gran told me to watch carefully so that I could do it myself the next day. "With any luck, it'll be gone in a day or two if we do it thoroughly tonight and then again in the morning. And see if you can find a few minutes during the day to give it another little massage. It's not a bad sprain, otherwise you wouldn't be able to walk at all."

"But will I be able to do gym tomorrow?"

"Better not. You don't want to ruin your foot for the competition."

"Do you think it'll be better in time for the competition though?"

"I'll cross my fingers."

I gulped and went into a daydream, wondering what to say to Miss Banner. But Gran's voice brought me back. "Do you think Miss Coralie's right?"

"What, about having to choose between ballet and gym?"

She nodded.

"Yes...because the older I get the more extra gym I'll have to do. There are so many competitions, you see."

"And I presume you don't want to quit it."

"Well, everyone says I'm really good at it."

"That isn't what I asked. Why do you think Miss Coralie wants you to make a decision? Why doesn't she just let you keep taking ballet for fun and not worry too much if you forget where you are every so often? What's wrong with that?"

"Because she's fed up about the gym making me do everything wrong."

"But why should she mind so much?"

I didn't get what Gran was trying to say. I shook my head slowly. "I don't know why."

"It's because she can see how good you are at ballet, and she's sad and angry because it looks as though you're going to specialize in gym. I expect Miss Coralie was hoping you might specialize in ballet. There was no need for her to say anything at all, was there? But she wanted to know how you were feeling."

I couldn't believe what Gran was saying. "Do you really think Miss Coralie thinks I'm good?"

"Yes. And she's right. You *are* good. I saw you in the show, and since then I've seen you practicing and improving. I've patted myself on the back lots of times for getting you those lessons."

I just stared at the table and did some more thinking. It still brought me back to the same problem. "The trouble is, I've got too much gym all the time, and it's probably going to get more and more... But I don't want to give it up, and I *definitely* don't want to give up ballet."

"How does gym make you feel?"

"Really good. Like being on a fast ride at a theme park. At least...it used to..."

"*Used* to?"

I nodded.

Gran patted my leg. "Go and see how that foot feels now."

I went over to her windowsill taking careful steps, but on the third step I realized that I didn't have to worry. It was much better. Carefully I tried a *plié* and then a *rond de jambe* and then I came away from the windowsill and slowly raised my left leg in a low *arabesque*.

"How does it feel?"

"Lots better!"

"Good. Now, forget about your foot and tell me how the dancing made you feel?"

"I can't explain."

"Why not?"

"Because it's not like anything else. It's just...the best feeling in the whole world."

Gran looked at me with searching eyes and it was a moment before she spoke. "I never *did* tell you what happened to my long, straight, smooth-flowing river, did I?"

"No, and I've been dying to find out. Has it got something to do with ballet and gym, maybe?"

"Well..."

9 The Competition

My foot was much better the next day. It still hurt some if I tried out a *changement* or anything jumpy, but whenever the teacher wasn't watching I did a bit of the massaging thing that Gran had taught me. All the same, I didn't dare do gym and I knew Miss Banner was not going to be pleased.

"I don't know how I did it, Miss Banner... It just started hurting, and I don't want to strain it..."

"Hmm, well *I* can guess how you did it. I've warned you often enough about ballet, Rose." She shook her head and huffed and puffed as she looked at my feet and did the same massage that Gran had taught me. "Keep doing this at home and *no* ballet! Come and see me tomorrow, all right?"

I nodded. She could say what she liked about ballet, because Gran had sorted out the confusion in my head, so I just smiled and said nothing.

By the following Monday, my foot was completely better. On Tuesday morning I told Mom I didn't want to go to ballet because I wanted to save all my energy and concentration for the gym competition.

"Sensible girl!" said Mom.

"Wonders will never cease!" said Dad.

"What time does the competition start on Saturday?" asked Rory.

"Two o'clock," said Mom.

"Do *I* have to go?" asked Adam for the tenth time.

"We'll see," said Mom.

✳

In the end, Adam did go. And at ten past three on Saturday afternoon, I was with Miss Banner and Sasha and Katie and all the other competitors from the other schools at one end of the massive sports hall. Mom and Dad and Gran were with Adam, Rory and Jack and the rest of the audience at the other end.

I was dying for the competition to start now and I think the audience was too. Everyone had stopped talking, silently waiting for the first vault. I wasn't at all nervous. In fact, I think Poppy and Jasmine were more nervous than me. They'd come running over when we were right in the middle of the warm-up and done a quick thumb-thumb, because Jasmine said that Poppy had been worrying that the last one we'd done hadn't been a good one, because our thumbs hadn't been totally touching, and she didn't want to be the one to bring me bad luck.

We had to do two vaults each. Miss Banner had decided that Sasha would go first. I was going to go last and my two vaults were a straddle and a handspring. Handsprings are the hardest, so they're rated on a scale of one to ten. All the other types of vault are rated on a scale of eight. But not many people risk handsprings because they're easier to mess up, so you might only get a score of six or seven points out of ten. Most gym teachers think it's best to stick to the easier vaults and try to get eight out of eight.

Our school was the last school to do the vaults and I was the very last person of all. Out of all the competitors only one other girl had done a handspring, but she'd slightly messed up the landing and only scored a six. The best school so far was Little Trent. All three girls had scored perfect eights for both their vaults. So they'd scored forty-eight points, which was the best so far.

The moment I realized that, I started to get

nervous. It was strange because I'm never usually nervous about anything. It made my shoulders go stiff and I had to keep rolling them around and around to get them loose again.

My nervousness disappeared when I was in my start position. I just wanted to get on with it. I ran hard and gave it lots of attack on the vault, and the landing felt fine. As I did my presentation at the end the audience clapped and I wondered if their hands were beginning to hurt because they'd had to do so much clapping. I was so busy thinking about that as I walked back up to the start that I forgot to look at the judges' mark, so I had to ask Miss Banner what it was when I got back.

"You scored eight, Rose! Well done!"

A moment later, Sasha was pounding toward the vault for the second time. I heard Miss Banner whisper "Yes!" to herself as Sasha went into her straddle, and then a bigger "Yess!" when the audience applauded her landing.

Sasha and Katie both scored eights and then it was my turn again. I did my starting presentation and imagined I was giving myself an injection of *oomph*, then set off really fast. The feeling I had, as I did my flight off, was as good as being on a roller coaster. I flung my arms back hard and didn't wobble at all as the clapping started.

"Yessss!" came a loud voice from the audience and I realized it was Adam. He was clapping over his head and so was Rory. Jack was stabbing the air to make me look at the judges. I couldn't believe my eyes. They were holding up a nine. We were even with Little Trent now. I looked back at the audience and saw Mom half-laughing and half-crying and Dad gave me a big thumbs up. Poppy and Jasmine were so busy thumb-thumbing each other that they didn't even see me looking. And Gran was beaming. She gave me a little wave and I gave her one back.

After that it was the floor work. The schools had to go in the same order and we were all using the same music. I thought the first school did a really good routine because they made it lovely and floaty, but the judges only gave them a six.

Miss Banner spoke to me in an urgent hiss. "You know why that school was marked down, don't you?"

"Because it was too much like ballet?"

"Exactly!"

"Well, if I'd been a judge I would have given them ten," I told her.

Katie and Sasha giggled but Miss Banner didn't look very pleased. "Make sure you don't start softening the movements when it's our turn, Rose, that's all!"

I wasn't going to soften them. I didn't want to. This was gym, not ballet. I was going to be straight and strong with parallel lines and no turnout.

The second and third schools both scored eight and Little Trent scored nine. It was no wonder because they had really difficult skills in their routine and I didn't see a single thing go wrong.

"I would have given *them* ten, too," I told Miss Banner.

"It's a good job you're not the judge then, because that would make them impossible to beat!"

"Oh! I hadn't thought of that!" And I hadn't.

The fifth school scored seven and then it was our turn. Just before the music started, when Sasha, Katie and I were in our positions, you could hear all kinds of sounds that you'd never normally notice. They came out loudly against the silence. I knew I shouldn't be thinking about things like that because it stopped me from focusing. So I pretended to be injecting myself with *oomph* again and then the music started. Katie didn't seem at all nervous any more. She'd already told me that she likes it better when it's all three of us because then she doesn't feel as though it's her fault if it goes wrong.

But we didn't go wrong. In fact, I think we did it better than we'd ever done it before and when I landed in the splits and the other two were in their finishing positions, the audience cheered and whistled as well as clapping. Well, there was *one* whistle – I think it was Dad actually.

We didn't have to wait at all for the judges to give their mark. They just looked at each other, nodded and held up a ten. I heard another gasp, only this time it came from me! We'd won! We'd actually won! It was unbelievable!

And now it was all over we were allowed to do what we wanted. We didn't have to behave correctly because it didn't matter any more. Sasha and Katie were jumping up and down hugging each other and trying to get me to join in the hug. I joined in for a few seconds, then I went toward the audience and Poppy and

Jasmine came rushing down so we three could do our own hug.

"You were the best, Rose!" said Jasmine. "I mean, I already knew you were brilliant, but I've never seen you in a real competiton and I couldn't believe all those things you can do."

And then Miss Banner came over. "Well done, Rose. You were so strong and so focused all the way through." She looked up into the audience. "Here comes your family. My goodness, you've got a lot of fans, haven't you!"

"This is my Gran," I told Miss Banner, holding Gran's hand and pulling her forward because she was stuck behind Jack.

"Pleased to meet you," said Miss Banner.

I looked around and saw that the whole of the floor area was full of gymnasts and audience all mixed up. The talking was loud and excited because the final marks had been put up on the wall and everyone could see that our school had won.

"Something of a star, you are, Rose!" said Dad, winking at Miss Banner.

"She certainly is," said Miss Banner. "That hard work paid off, didn't it, Rose?" She put her arm around me. "And the next competition should be even better, with all the extra classes."

Mom hugged me. "Well done, honey!"

"We'll have you in those Olympic Games yet!" laughed Dad.

"I bet you *could*, you know Ro!" said Adam, and Jack and Rory both started agreeing with him.

I looked at Gran. Her eyes were twinkling, just like they had done when she'd told me about the long, straight river. I suddenly knew that now was the time for me to say something.

"I don't want to be in the Olympic Games, Adam."

Everyone looked at me. Miss Banner laughed. "Well, not just yet, anyway!"

That made everyone laugh.

"No, not ever."

"How about the European Games then?" said Dad.

This time, no one laughed. I think they must have seen the serious look on my face. I caught sight of Jasmine's huge eyes. I'd told her and Poppy how I felt and what I was going to say when the time came and they'd both hugged me and said I was so brave. I didn't feel brave. I just felt right because nothing was mixed up in my head any more. I could still hear Gran's voice inside my head telling me about the long, straight, smooth-flowing river that was her life, and how it all changed when she was seventeen.

"I suddenly knew in my heart that I wasn't good enough to be a ballerina and if I couldn't be a ballerina, I didn't want to have anything more to do with ballet. Everyone said I'd regret it, and tried to persuade me to be a teacher, and talked about what a waste of time my ballet lessons had been. But I knew they hadn't.

They'd been the river of my life – the long, straight, smooth-flowing river, but the river was branching into two and the ballet part was turning into a stream that would become more a gentle backwater. Somewhere beautiful, that would always be a haven, but no longer part of the main stream of my life. Your grandad came along shortly after that. He was the biggest stream of all and he stayed with me for longer than any other stream.

Your river, dear, was a long, straight gym river, until the ballet stream came along to join it. But you don't need anyone to tell you which is more important to you. All you have to do is close your eyes and feel the pull of the current and then you'll know. Just like I did."

I turned to Miss Banner. "I don't want to do any more competitions, Miss Banner. I really like gym and I don't want to give it up, but I don't like it as much as I like ballet, so I only want to do gym club from now on."

All over the hall the hubbub of people talking and laughing went on, but in our little circle there was a horrible silence. No one liked what I'd said. I began to feel nervous and I looked at Gran to make sure that I hadn't been rude or anything. Her eyes were still twinkling and it made my nervousness go away. Then Poppy and Jasmine came and stood on either side of me. The triplegang together.

Adam was first to speak. "You're crazy!"

"Totally nuts," added Rory.

"Well, I think it's cool," said Jack. "Let her do what she wants."

"No one's going to make you do extra gym if you don't want to, honey," said Mom. But there was a sad look in her eyes.

Dad was frowning. "You'd be a fool to waste that talent, Rose."

"Well, we can cross that bridge when we come to it," said Miss Banner, smiling brightly. "I must go over and say hello to Sasha's and

Katie's families now."

I don't think she believed that I meant what I'd just said. Or maybe she thought I'd change my mind by the time it came to the next competition. But I wouldn't. I was certain of that. In fact, I'd never been so certain of anything in my whole life.

Gran winked at me and I remembered what she'd said when she'd come up to say night-night to me.

"You see, you ARE like that Russian doll, dear. You had so much inside you, and now you're starting to find it all!"

10 The Best Feeling in the World

"And *one* and *two* and *three* and *four*..."

I was wearing my lovely new leotard that Gran had bought me, and I felt like a bird that had been trapped in a cage and was now flying around the sky. No way could a roller coaster ever feel this good. We were doing the *port de bras* and it was wonderful to be using soft arms. Poppy and Jasmine had helped me a lot with this exercise and I knew I was doing it better than I'd ever done it before.

At the beginning of the lesson Miss Coralie had asked me if I was better now after missing class last week, and I'd told her that I hadn't been sick, I'd just had too much gym to do for the competition. She'd asked me how I'd gotten on in the competition and I'd told her that our school had won.

"Wonderful! Well done!" she'd said, but I'd seen that same sad look in her eyes that I'd seen in Mom's.

"*Tendu* to second and close in fifth..." Miss Coralie had been walking along the rows but she stopped in front of me and watched me till we'd finished on the first side, then said, "Nice, Rose," and kept watching me while we all did it on the other side.

"You've been working hard," she said, when the music finished. Her eyes were very bright.

"It's because the competition's over so now I'm back to ballet."

"Until the next competition?" she said quietly.

"I'm not doing any more competitions. I thought about what you said and I've made my decision. I want to concentrate on ballet."

She smiled a real smile and several girls stared at me. Then we went on to the next exercise just as if nothing had happened. Miss Coralie stood at the front and watched the class. I loved doing the *arabesque*. I'd worked hard at getting my placing exactly right and I could feel Miss Coralie's eyes on me again. Everything just flowed and flowed until I held my final position and heard the best words in the world.

"Lovely, Rose!"

The feeling was so big, I thought it might burst out of me, but I was determined to hold it tight inside until I passed Jazz and Poppy in the line.

I couldn't wait to see the looks on their faces when I told them.

The End

Turn the page to find out more
about all the special ballet steps
that Poppy, Jasmine and Rose
learn in Miss Coralie's classes...

Basic Ballet Positions

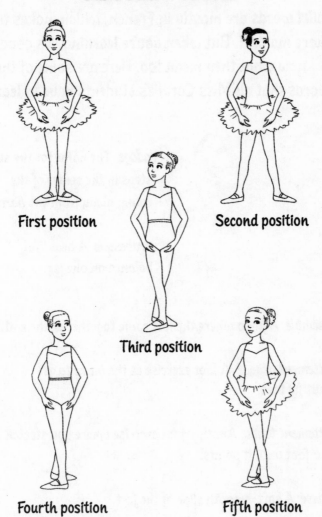

First position

Second position

Third position

Fourth position

Fifth position

Ballet words are mostly in French, which makes them more magical. But when you're learning, it's good to know what they mean too. Here are some of the words that all Miss Coralie's students have to learn:

adage The name for the slow steps in the center of the room, away from the *barre*.

arabesque A beautiful balance on one leg.

assemblé A jump where the feet come together at the end.

battement dégagé A foot exercise at the *barre* to get beautiful toes.

battement tendu Another foot exercise where you stretch your foot until it points.

chassé A soft, smooth slide of the feet.

echappé This one's impossible to describe, but it's like your feet escaping from each other!

fifth position croisé When you are facing, say the *left* corner, with your feet in fifth position, and your front foot is the *right* foot.

fouetté This step is so fast your feet are in a blur! You do it to prepare for *pirouettes*.

grand battement High kick!

jeté A spring where you land on the opposite foot. Rose loves these!

pas de bourrée Tiny little steps to the side, like a mouse.

pas de chat A cat hop from one foot to the other.

plié This is the first step we do in class. You have to bend your knees slowly and make sure your feet are turned right out, with your heels firmly planted on the floor for as long as possible.

port de bras Arm movements, which Poppy is good at.

révérence The curtsy at the end of class.

rond de jambe This is where you make a circle with your leg.

sissonne A scissor step.

sissonne en arrière A scissor step going backward. This is really hard!

sissonne en avant A scissor step going forward.

soubresaut A jump off two feet, pointing your feet hard in the air.

temps levé A step and sweep up the other leg then jump.

turnout You have to stand with your legs and feet and hips all opened out and pointing to the side, not the front. This is the most important thing in ballet that everyone learns right from the start.

Dancing Friends

3 GREAT STORIES IN 1

Follow Poppy, Jasmine and Rose
as they dance ever closer to their
ballerina dreams...

Poppy has the chance of dancing in a show, but will
she push herself too far? Will Jasmine get to audition
for the world-famous Royal Ballet School? And can
Rose keep out of trouble and let her star quality
shine through?

Three more classic stories in
one enchanting collection:
Dancing Princess
Dancing with the Stars
Dancing Forever

9780794517410
$7.99

The Christmas Nutcracker

Poppy, Jasmine and Rose are so excited.
Their ballerina dreams have come true and they are
dancing in The Nutcracker with a real professional
ballet company. It should be a magical time but the
rehearsals are tough and some of the other dancers
are less than friendly. The three girls are also
missing their wonderful teacher, Miss Coralie,
who is sick in hospital.

Will their dancing still shine on Christmas Eve?

9780794513696
$4.99

Also by Ann Bryant

Billie and the Parent Plan

Billie just knows she's going to be teased to death about her boring, bald stepdad. But worse than that – with a phony new stepsister and a mom who hardly seems to notice her now, Billie doesn't feel like she belongs in her own family any more. So she figures out a great idea: The Parent Plan. All she needs is to get adopted into a new family – easy! Or not...

A warm and sparkingly funny novel about families, friends and fitting in.

9780794517212

$4.99

About the author

Ann Bryant trained as a ballet dancer until she was seventeen and went on to teach music, dance and drama to children. She has now built a career as a children's author and a music educationalist, with eighty books published, as well as scripts, poetry, songs and stories broadcast on BBC Schools Radio.

Ann has two grown-up daughters and lives with her husband in Kent, England. She values family and friends more than anything, but also loves going to the theater, the cinema, the gym and riding her bicycle.

To find out more about Ann Bryant visit her website: www.annbryant.co.uk